W9-BXX-144

"Excuse me..."

Kit whirled toward the soft voice, stubbing his toe against his chair in the process. Swearing softly, he stumbled to his desk, causing his phone and answering machine to crash to the floor.

In the midst of the chaos, all Kit could do was stare. Straddling the threshold between his own office and his secretary's was a gorgeous woman, one who could have graced the pages of any P.I. novel, including his own.

Here she is. That was the only clear thought Kit had as the tingling in the back of his neck morphed into an electric current. The tingling he understood. He'd been expecting something all day, and she was it. Definitely. And he understood the tightening in his gut. He'd experienced it before, but never to this extent— that instant sexual awareness. The sensation of the ground shifting under his feet? Now, that was tougher to explain. But hey, this was San Francisco. It could be a tremor.

And then it finally registered. The sexy female standing in his doorway was wearing a suit— *that was covered with blood....*

Blaze™

Dear Reader,

When my editor suggested I write a miniseries about three Greek brothers who are TALL, DARK...AND DANGEROUSLY HOT, I jumped at the chance!

I decided that the brothers would be a P.I., a cop and a defense attorney, and that their stories would be set on one steamy hot weekend when all three Angelis brothers would be caught up in the same mystery involving star-crossed lovers, feuding families, murder and greed.

For Kit Angelis, Friday has been one of those days when anything that could go wrong has. His one goal is to clear his desk so that he can get away for a weekend. But before he makes his escape, a pretty blonde walks into his office. For a man who loves solving a mystery, the lady is simply irresistible. Her suit is covered in blood, she's carrying a wedding dress in a bag over her arm and she claims that she can't remember who she is. But the real kicker for Kit is that, runaway bride or not, he "senses" his mystery client might be the one woman the fates have chosen for him....

I hope you'll come along for the ride as Kit and his mystery woman discover more than they've bargained for. And I hope that you'll want to continue the adventure with Nik (*The Cop*) in July and Theo (*The Defender*) in August.

For more information about the Angelis brothers visit my Web site, www.carasummers.com.

Happy reading!

Cara Summers

THE P.I.
Cara Summers

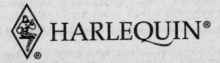

HARLEQUIN®

TORONTO • NEW YORK • LONDON
AMSTERDAM • PARIS • SYDNEY • HAMBURG
STOCKHOLM • ATHENS • TOKYO • MILAN • MADRID
PRAGUE • WARSAW • BUDAPEST • AUCKLAND

If you purchased this book without a cover you should be aware that this book is stolen property. It was reported as "unsold and destroyed" to the publisher, and neither the author nor the publisher has received any payment for this "stripped book."

ISBN-13: 978-0-373-79334-1
ISBN-10:   0-373-79334-0

THE P.I.

Copyright © 2007 by Carolyn Hanlon.

All rights reserved. Except for use in any review, the reproduction or utilization of this work in whole or in part in any form by any electronic, mechanical or other means, now known or hereafter invented, including xerography, photocopying and recording, or in any information storage or retrieval system, is forbidden without the written permission of the publisher, Harlequin Enterprises Limited, 225 Duncan Mill Road, Don Mills, Ontario, Canada M3B 3K9.

This is a work of fiction. Names, characters, places and incidents are either the product of the author's imagination or are used fictitiously, and any resemblance to actual persons, living or dead, business establishments, events or locales is entirely coincidental.

This edition published by arrangement with Harlequin Books S.A.

® and TM are trademarks of the publisher. Trademarks indicated with ® are registered in the United States Patent and Trademark Office, the Canadian Trade Marks Office and in other countries.

www.eHarlequin.com

Printed in U.S.A.

ABOUT THE AUTHOR

Cara Summers has written twenty-three books for Harlequin. Her stories have won several awards, including the Golden Leaf, the Award of Excellence and a W.I.S.H. and Reviewer's Choice Award from *Romantic Times BOOKreviews*. Cara loves writing for the Harlequin Blaze line. "I can write so many different kinds of stories—from forbidden fantasies and island flings to sexy Gothic romances. There's always something new to challenge me." But when her editor suggested she write a trilogy about three Greek brothers, she saw the potential for three incredible heroes...as well as a story line with a twist. And take it from Cara, "Kit, Nik and Theo Angelis are truly TALL, DARK...AND DANGEROUSLY HOT!

Books by Cara Summers

Don't miss any of our special offers. Write to us at the following address for information on our newest releases.

Harlequin Reader Service
U.S.: 3010 Walden Ave., P.O. Box 1325, Buffalo, NY 14269
Canadian: P.O. Box 609, Fort Erie, Ont. L2A 5X3

To the current men in my life—who all happen
to be brothers! I love you all!

To my sons—Kevin, Brian and Brendan
(You're lucky because, like the Angelis brothers,
you each have two brothers!)

To my grandson Andrew
(You're lucky, too, because you have a great sister!)

To my nephew Nick
(You're lucky enough to have two great sisters!)

To my nephews Ryan and Conor (I love you, too!)

And especially to my own brother, Andy
(You have two sisters, but we're the lucky ones!)

Prologue

IN THE TOWER ROOM on the top floor of her house, Cass Angelis sat at her rosewood desk and prepared to see the future.

Laurel leaves burned in a glass bowl, candlelight flickered on the walls and the music of Yolanda Kondonassis, the Greek harpist, flowed around her. Her ability as a seer came as naturally to Cass as gardening or cooking came to other women. In her younger years, she'd used her abilities to help anyone who came to her. It was only after her husband Demetrius's death that she'd begun to charge for her services, and over the last eighteen years, she'd built up enough of a reputation in the San Francisco area to make a comfortable living.

But tonight she had no client. Tonight her concern was for her family. Her son, Dino, who was serving his country in the Navy, her nephews, Nik, Theo and Kit, and her niece, Philly—she wasn't sure which one or ones the Fates would offer choices to. All she was sure of was that choices would be offered this weekend. The small china clock on the mantel read two minutes to midnight—the witching hour. Not that Cass was a witch, not by a long shot. She couldn't have whipped up a spell to save her life. But she did have insights into what the Fates might weave into a person's future.

Might weave because it was always up to the individual to embrace or try to escape their destiny.

Her gift of sight had been inherited from her great-grandmother, Ariel Andropoulis, who'd claimed that her powers could be traced all the way back to Apollo's Oracle at Delphi. Cass liked to believe that was true. On occasions like tonight she even burned laurel leaves the way Apollo's priestesses had. But the only thing she was certain of was that psychic powers ran in her family, especially in the females.

Her sister had possessed the ability to "see," too, and although Cass knew that Penelope had passed it on in some form to all four of her children, it was only Philly who acknowledged and used her gift.

Cass glanced at the latest family portrait that her nephews and niece had given her for her birthday last month. She was in the same chair she sat in now. Her brother-in-law Spiro stood to her left. Philly sat on the arm of the chair and Nik, Theo and Kit stood behind and to her right. Dino hadn't been there for the photo. Currently, he was stationed in the Gulf. All of the Angelis men loved the sea, but Dino had been most susceptible to its lure. From when he was a little boy, she'd sensed that one day he would leave, so she hadn't been surprised when he'd applied to Annapolis.

Cass continued to study the family photo. The Angelis men were all beautiful—tall, dark and handsome, just as her husband, Demetrius, had been and, for just a moment, she allowed herself to drift backward to the past.

When she and Penelope had graduated from high

school, their father had taken them to Greece. He'd intended to put them in touch with their heritage, but she and Penelope had "known" that the visit to Greece would offer them much more.

Cass's mind filled with images of Ionic columns, marble statues and theatres built into sloping hillsides. Although she and Penelope had been fascinated by the history, the culture and the literature of the country, it had been the sea that had drawn them the most. They'd dragged their father to just about every fishing village along the coast, and it had been in one of them that they'd met Spiro and Demetrius Angelis.

For both her sister and herself, it had been a case of love at first sight. Still, Cass wasn't certain that she and Penelope would have had the courage to grab what the Fates had offered them. Luckily, the two Angelis brothers had taken the decision out of their hands by following them back to San Francisco. With her father's help, they'd opened their own restaurant, The Poseidon. For a time, Cass had known what it was like to love and be truly loved in return.

With a sigh, she shifted her gaze to a picture of Demetrius. She knew all too well that the Fates were fickle. What they gave could be snatched away at any time, but even in the worst of times, they offered unexpected gifts.

Spiro, his children and Dino had been her family since that day nearly eighteen years ago when Demetrius and Penelope had lost their lives in a boating accident. Nik, her oldest nephew, had been twelve, the same age as Dino. Theo had been eleven, Kit ten and little Philly had been only four. Spiro had been left with the restaurant to run all on his own. So her father had invited them all to move into his house, and she'd taken over the job of raising Penelope's and Spiro's children along with her son.

Cass smiled. Her sadness had been followed by unexpected joy, as she'd come to look upon Penelope's children as her own. At some point in the wink of time, the Angelis boys had become men. Her gaze returned to the photo of her husband Demetrius. And at least one of them was about to find the love of his life just as she had.

Maybe that was why she'd been thinking of Demetrius. It would happen this weekend—if they chose to take what the Fates offered them.

The first stroke of midnight brought Cass out of her reverie. Taking a deep breath, she put away the odd sense of loneliness that she'd been feeling lately and lifted her crystals. Light from a full moon streamed through tall, narrow windows and the milky mist in the faceted jewels began to swirl. She often saw things more clearly at that magic moment when one day gave way to the next. When the clock chimed again, the shadows in the stones broke into colors—a rainbow of them. They warmed her palms, and slowly, colors shifted, parted, then bled into one another until an image formed in her mind—a young woman, small and blonde with bottle-green eyes. And she was racing down a shadowed flight of stairs. In a holy place? Before Cass could get a real sense of the surroundings or the circumstances, the colors shifted again, and this time it was Kit, her youngest nephew, she saw. The young woman was at his side and they were both running through the darkness. This time she sensed danger.

Closing her eyes, Cass tried to see beyond the images to what they meant. A damsel in distress for Kit. The Fates had chosen wisely, she thought. Her youngest nephew, the dreamer, had always had an errant-knight streak in him.

Even as joy streamed through her, her heart squeezed a bit. Kit would be the first of her children to meet the woman he was fated for. From the time he was small, Kit had always been insatiably curious, and that characteristic had often gotten him into scrapes. It had also shaped him for his future careers as a P.I. and a crime-fiction writer. Her lips curved slightly. The boy just couldn't resist solving puzzles. Yes, a damsel in distress would do very well.

Shifting her attention back to the swirling colors in the crystals, Cass moved them in her hands and watched the rainbows grow darker and darker until everything was gray. Suddenly, a flash of fire knifed through the darkness. Cass's heart chilled and her stomach tightened with fear. What she saw was money, guns and blood. What she sensed was greed, envy and death.

The crystals burned now against her skin. But she kept her gaze steady. Colors flashed again, shattering the darkness. And she sensed the love—passionate and true.

Would it be enough to protect her Kit and the woman the Fates had chosen for him?

1

Friday, August 28—evening

SHE SURFACED SLOWLY, her senses awakening one by one. She felt the pain first—a hammering headache near her right temple. And heat. Humid air pressed in on her carrying the scent of exhaust fumes and the noise of traffic. Engines thrummed and a horn blasted in a staccato rhythm.

Close by, voices shouted. Angry male voices. She caught enough of what they were saying to wonder if their language was turning the surrounding air blue.

Where was she? What had happened? Panic bubbled up as the questions swirled through her mind. Opening her eyes, she managed to get a glimpse of her surroundings before a fresh wave of pain had her wincing and squeezing them shut again. She'd registered enough to know that it was dark out. Not pitch-black, but a sort of twilight-gray. She was in a car. The plastic divider that separated her from the front seat made her think it had to be a taxi.

Opening her eyes again, she gritted her teeth against the pain and took more careful stock of her surroundings. She was half lying on the backseat. The shattered window to her right gave her the first clue that she'd been in an accident. And the two men right outside that window were arguing about who'd caused it.

Okay, she knew where she was—in a taxi. And that there'd been an accident. In the initial impact she must have hit her head and been knocked out for a few minutes. But she was conscious now. How badly had she been hurt?

As she began to lever herself into a sitting position, the pounding at her temple increased and had her gritting her teeth again. But she made it. So far, so good. She wasn't dizzy and she was almost getting used to the headache, which seemed to be the only source of pain.

"Bottom line. I had a green light. You ran a red," growled a gravelly voice to her right. "And I got a witness—my fare. Hey, lady, you want to tell this guy what happened?"

She carefully turned to look at the man whose round and mustached face had appeared at the broken window. He jabbed a finger at her. "Tell him I had the green light."

"I…can't." Panic did more than bubble this time. It shot through her in sharp arrows.

"What do you mean, you can't? You saw it."

"I don't…remember." When she searched her mind for the details that had led up to the accident, she came up empty. She raised her hands and pressed her fingers against her temples, hoping that might help.

It didn't.

"What are you talking about?" he asked. "You yelled at me to look out, that this creep was running the red. And then you screamed." He jerked a thumb at the skinny man standing next to him. "He rammed right into us and caused a six-car pileup. Traffic is stopped in four directions."

She shifted her gaze back to the man who'd evidently

been driving her taxi, taking in more details now. He had thick dark hair, a stocky build and he wore a folded, red-print bandanna around his head that made him look like a pirate. If someone had thrust a Bible into her hand, she would have sworn that she'd never seen him before in her life.

She pressed a hand against her stomach. "Give me—" When her voice cracked, she swallowed hard. "I need a minute."

"Lady, are you all right?" It was the other man who spoke. He was tall with the thin build of a scarecrow, and she could hear concern in his voice.

"I'm fine," she said, stubbornly clinging to the hope that she was speaking the truth. But it wasn't merely the accident she didn't remember. She couldn't even recall getting into the taxi…or where she was going…or where she'd been…or…

She dropped her hands into her lap and clenched them into fists as the pain in her head sharpened.

She couldn't…she couldn't remember who she was.

"Look," the skinny man continued, "she's hurt. She's got blood on her. I'll call an ambulance."

Blood? As he punched numbers into his cell phone, she glanced down at herself. Sure enough, there were dark stains on the cuff of her jacket and on her skirt. She gingerly probed her right temple and located a goose egg just above it, but there was no sign of blood on her hand when she drew it away. Was she hurt somewhere else? She turned up her cuff, but there wasn't a mark on her arm. Nor could she find any kind of wound when she checked beneath the stains on her skirt. The only pain she was experiencing was a headache—which was getting worse.

"We got an ambulance coming, lady." It was her taxi

driver who spoke, and his earlier anger seemed to have faded. "You just sit tight. You're going to be all right."

"You're probably in shock," the other man assured her. "You just take it easy until they get here."

Shock. That had to be it. Relief streamed through her. Any minute now, her memory would come flooding back. And in the meantime… There had to be clues. She glanced around the backseat, looking for her purse. A white plastic dress bag was the first thing that caught her eye. It lay half on the seat to her left and half on the floor. She realized she'd been lying on it when she'd first regained consciousness. Instinctively, she lifted the bag, smoothing it as she hung it carefully on the hook over the door. Through a clear plastic panel on the front, she could make out a white lace gown embroidered with tiny seed pearls. A wedding dress?

Hers?

The momentary relief she'd felt was shoved out by a fresh wave of panic. Surely she'd remember if she were on the way to her wedding. But why would she be going to her own wedding in a taxi? Wouldn't she be with family?

Something knotted in her stomach. Maybe she didn't have a family.

She turned to the window. "Sir?" The word sounded like a squeak, and she swallowed hard when her taxi driver's face once more appeared in the window.

"You all right?" he asked.

"Yes," she lied. "Where did you pick me up?"

He frowned at her. "You don't remember that, either?"

"No."

"She's in shock, I tell you," the skinny man said. "Don't give her a hard time. Just tell her where you picked her up."

Her taxi driver let out a disgusted sigh. "You flagged me down on Bellevue."

"And where did I ask you to take me?"

His frown deepened, but he reached in through the passenger window and extracted a clipboard. "503 Lathrop. It's just two blocks down on the right-hand side. We were almost there when this idiot ran the light."

"Did not," the skinny man muttered.

Ignoring him, her driver handed her a business card. "You gave me this when you got in the car."

She glanced down and read the neatly printed name. *Kristophe Angelis, Private Investigations.* Beneath that in smaller font was an address—503 Lathrop. She read the phone number, too. Nothing on the card rang a bell. As far as she knew, she'd never seen the name before.

The sound of sirens in the distance had the two men turning away from the window, and she was grateful for their distraction. She had to think, to take stock of her situation.

She hadn't called the taxi; she'd flagged it down. And she had a wedding dress. There were bloodstains on her suit. And she'd given the taxi driver the business card of a private investigator. The knot in her stomach tightened. No matter how you tried to add it up, it wasn't good.

Maybe she wasn't on the way *to* her wedding. She could be a runaway bride. That seemed a more plausible explanation for why she was alone in a taxi with her wedding dress. She'd had a case of bridal jitters.

But why was she running to a P.I.? Her gaze dropped to her suit again. A runaway bride with blood on her suit? That was not good. Her fingers tightened on the business card. Maybe this Kristophe Angelis would know who she was.

The sirens grew louder.

"It's the ambulance," the skinny man said.

"Naw," her taxi driver corrected. "It's the police. They'll interview a few witnesses and find out you ran that red light."

"I had the green."

"*I* had the green. My fare will tell the police that—as soon as she comes out of shock."

Police. The word sent a chill through her, and she dropped her gaze once more to the bloodstains on her skirt. They'd want to know how the blood got there. How could she explain that to the police when she couldn't remember?

Maybe she didn't want to remember.

But she had to. Moving to the edge of the seat, she peered down at the floor of the taxi. She did have a purse, didn't she? She'd glimpsed black leather when she'd moved the dress bag. Relief streamed through her. Surely, there'd be answers in there. It was heavy and it took some effort to drag it onto her lap. Opening it, she peered at the contents.

She hadn't thought the knot in her stomach could twist any tighter, but she'd been wrong. Even in the dim light, she could recognize the gleam of metal and make out the shape of a gun. Beneath it lay bundles of bills. The ones she could see on top were twenties.

It was a lot of money. Doing her best to avoid touching the gun, she slipped her hand into the tote, sliding it down the sides of the stacked bills and trying to locate a wallet or anything else that might tell her who she was. But she came up empty.

"You remember anything yet?"

She started, clutching the tote closed before turning to see her taxi driver peering in the window. "No. Sorry."

"Shit," he muttered as he turned and walked away.

She could see beyond him to where two uniformed officers were talking to the tall, skinny man. A small crowd had gathered on the sidewalk. Even as she watched, one of the policemen pulled a notebook out of his pocket and started to talk to the bystanders.

This was her chance, she thought. If she stayed here, she was going to have to explain the blood, the gun, the wedding dress and the small fortune in money in a tote bag. And she couldn't. She slipped one twenty out of a bundle and set it on the seat. The money might not be hers, but she didn't want to leave the taxi driver without his fare. Then keeping her eye on the two policemen, she very carefully opened the door that hadn't suffered damage from the accident. She gathered up the tote and the wedding dress and slipped away into the crowd.

2

SETTLING HIMSELF at his desk, Kit Angelis opened his laptop and tried to ignore the tingling sensation at the back of his neck that always warned him something was about to happen. According to his aunt Cass, the sensation was a sign of Kit's innate psychic ability, a gift of premonition that Aunt Cass believed could be traced all the way back to ancient Greece. While the idea appealed to his imagination, Kit wasn't all that comfortable with the notion that he might be able to "see" into the future. He'd always preferred to take life as it came at him. It was challenging enough to deal with problems as they arose without having to handle the ones that were headed at him from the future.

Still, he took a moment to rub the back of his neck. The intensity of the tingling and the way that it had been building all day warned him that some significant event was looming on the horizon. In his opinion, these little premonitions didn't prove he was psychic. After all, no one had labeled his friend, Roman, a "seer" when he'd claimed he had a "feeling" that something was going to happen the night he'd crashed his father's car after Kit had talked his reluctant friend into taking it for a joyride.

Of course, his aunt's counterargument to that would be that Roman wasn't Greek. And Kit Angelis was—

certainly enough to know that something was definitely coming tonight.

No matter that it was the last thing he needed. He already had plans for the weekend. He was going fishing with his brothers.

For one tempting moment, he considered turning off his computer and hightailing it out of town. But the escape attempt would be futile. Fate had a way of dogging a person's footsteps. How often had Aunt Cass read the story of *Oedipus Rex* to him as a child? If good old King Oed hadn't been able to escape what the Fates had in store for him, how in the world did Kit Angelis hope to do it?

With a sigh, Kit pressed the button that would boot up his computer. When his dog Ari echoed his sigh, he glanced over to where the large black animal was stretched out below the window. The dog gave him a patient, long-suffering look.

"Working on it," he said as he reached into his bottom drawer and fished out a biscuit. "Twenty pages and then we're out of here." That was his goal—to get down the second chapter of his new novel. Then they'd leave. "I promise."

Ari made a sound in his throat. The tone sounded skeptical.

Kit aimed the biscuit for a spot right between the dog's paws and hit his mark. Ari would move for food, but not much else when the temperature was this humid, and Kit hadn't the heart to make the dog run for a treat.

Then he turned his attention back to the computer. He'd set his goal and he was going to accomplish it. True, this was not the way he'd envisioned spending a Friday evening— especially not one that was kicking off a long holiday weekend that he still intended to spend fishing with his brothers.

It wasn't merely psychic senses that ran strong in the Angelis family; he and his brothers had also inherited an affinity for the sea. His grandfather on his father's side had been a fisherman in Greece. His grandfather and great grandfather on his mother's side had been shipbuilders near Sausalito.

His oldest brother, Nik, especially loved the challenge of pitting himself against the elements, and so he'd be taking out his sailboat at some point this weekend. Theo would probably take the boat out, too, and he would definitely sit on the dock and throw his line in, but Kit sensed that Theo only participated in either activity because he just loved to be near water.

But for Kit, as well as for his father, the lure of the sea had always had to do with fishing. He just loved the game of it. In his mind, he pictured himself choosing one of the lures his father made, throwing his line out into the water and then waiting for that first tug that signaled the beginning of the battle.

Kit gave himself a mental shake. Twenty pages, he reminded himself. Of course, finishing them could mean that Theo and Nik would beat him to the cabin. He tried to ignore the stab of regret he felt about that as he opened up the file on his laptop. When the phone rang, he let the answering machine pick it up.

"Hey, bro, I know you're there."

It was Theo's voice. Some people thought that he and his brothers sounded alike, but Theo's drawl was unmistakable. His older brother always spoke slowly, the way he seemed to do everything else. Energy conservation, he called it. Whatever it was, his easy manner endeared him to juries and often deceived his opponents. Theo's mind worked fast enough, and he could move like lightning when the need arose. Like today, Kit thought with a frown. He was certain that Theo was calling to gloat because he'd arrived first at the cabin.

"Just thought you'd like to know," Theo continued, "I'm here. There's an hour or so of daylight left, so I think I'll get Dad's latest lure and catch me some fish."

Kit grimaced. He could picture his brother all too clearly in his mind, and it was just like Theo to mention the lure. Kit had been looking forward to using it. Theo knew that, just as Kit knew that Theo probably wouldn't even get his line wet. He'd just sit there on the porch and commune with the sea gods while he plotted strategy for his next case in court.

"Drive safely. No need to rush."

Kit stifled a sigh as he glanced at his watch. Theo must have clocked out at 5:00 p.m. on the dot. His only consolation was that his oldest brother Nik would be getting the same gloating message on his cell.

Ever since they were kids, they'd had an ongoing competition. Whoever made it through the cabin door first got their choice of poles and lures—and their father had quite a collection. When they were little, the race to the cabin had started the moment they'd rocketed out of the car. In the early days, Nik and Theo had had an advantage because they were older. As the youngest, he'd had to rely on wit and cunning. When he was six, he'd managed to tie their shoelaces together once. He could still recall the unadulterated joy he'd felt as he'd left them face down in the grass and sprinted for the cabin door.

Their dad still told that story in the restaurant he ran in the Fisherman's Wharf area—The Poseidon. In the Angelis family, fishing had always been something the men of the family did together—much to the annoyance of Philly, their kid sister. Kit's lips curved at the memory of the time that Philly had stowed away in the trunk of their father's car so that she could be a part of a fishing trip. She'd gotten her way—but only after she'd promised Spiro that she'd never do anything that dangerous again. His father told *that* story in the restaurant, too.

Usually, their father joined them. But ever since Spiro had lured the beautiful Helena Lambis from Greece and convinced her to open an upscale dining room on the upper level of The Poseidon, he seemed to find it very difficult to get away from work.

Philly was sure the relationship between his father and Helena was a romantic one. Helena had been a five-star chef at a hotel in Athens. When Spiro had visited Greece six months ago, he'd stayed at that very hotel. To hear Philly tell it, the story had overtones of Paris snatching Helen and carrying her off to Troy.

Spiro's version was less romantic. According to his father, his relationship with Helena was business. He'd been thinking for some time of opening a fine-dining restaurant on the upper level of The Poseidon and he'd convinced Helena to join him in that venture. But in the five months since Helena had established her restaurant, even their business relationship had become a bit rocky. The two had become competitors, each trying to outdo the other.

Whatever the true story was, Spiro seldom had time for fishing anymore. So Kit would be spending time with Nik and Theo, something that was becoming rarer since they all had very active careers.

Nik was a detective in the SFPD and on the fast track to becoming a captain. Theo had established a reputation as a top-notch criminal defense attorney in the area and, more recently, he'd been proclaimed one of the top ten most eligible bachelors by the *San Francisco Examiner,* something that had garnered him quite a bit of razzing from his brothers.

The article had also resulted in some "groupies," who'd followed Theo around for a time. When one of them had turned into a stalker, Theo had handled the situation with his usual unruffled aplomb, but he'd taken a bullet for his troubles and Kit had a hunch that there was a lot about the experience that he hadn't shared with them.

Kit glanced down at his laptop. His own career had taken off recently, too. For the past several months, he'd been juggling two jobs—his P.I. business, which paid the bills, and his new job as a published author. He'd signed a contract for two mystery novels just over a year ago. The first, which featured a Hitchcock-type hero with amnesia, had hit the bookshelves in the spring. The proposal and chapters for his second book were due in three weeks.

Nothing was going to keep him from achieving his goal. Not the images of his brothers arriving ahead of him at the cabin, not the soulful, pleading looks that Ari was giving him, not even the Fates, who'd thrown one obstacle after another in his path today.

First, there'd been a case that had dragged on late into the afternoon. He'd been typing up his report when a violent little summer storm had rolled through and driven his already ailing air conditioner into cardiac arrest. He'd jimmied open the window in the hopes that the storm had cooled the air, but it hadn't. Now, thanks to the heat wave that had been holding San Francisco in a tight fist for the past five days, the temperature in his office resembled a steam bath.

To top it off, he couldn't get the window to shut, so not only did he have to put up with the distracting sounds of traffic, but he was also being plagued by an occasional rogue breeze gusting in and scattering his once carefully stacked notes hither and yon.

Kit gave the mess of papers littering the floor of his office a considering look. Cleaning it up was probably a good idea. And he'd be more comfortable if he shed his blazer. With a sigh, he rose and stripped down to his T-shirt and jeans. As he toed his shoes off and peeled out of damp socks, he doggedly ignored the trickles of sweat rolling down his back. Moving to the center of his office, Kit squatted down and began to pick up papers and sort them into piles.

He could endure the heat. After all, the temperature hadn't been much better before the air conditioner had given up its ghost. The good news was that now his miserly landlord would be forced to replace the unit.

The phone rang again, and the tingling at the back of his neck once more claimed his attention. He stifled the urge to reach for the receiver as he listened to his voice inviting the caller to leave a message. It was probably Nik calling to gloat, too.

"Kit?"

The female voice was breathless. And frightened, Kit thought as he tried to place it.

"This is Sadie Oliver. You may not remember me. I'm Roman's—" A burst of static cut the last word off.

Though he'd only met her once, Kit remembered Sadie, all right. His friend Roman Oliver had two sisters. The younger one, Juliana, was about to start college. A year ago Sadie had graduated from Harvard Law School and come back home to work in her family's business. She was an attractive brunette, nearly as tall as Roman, and if she hadn't been his best friend's sister, he might have called her for a date. But his bond with Roman dated back to their freshman year in college when they'd shared a room.

He'd even dedicated his novel to him. Who better, since his friend had provided a wealth of information on the inner workings of organized-crime families. Not that the Oliver family had any connection to crime anymore. Their business holdings in real estate up and down the California coast had been legitimate ever since Roman's great-grandfather had moved to San Francisco and built his first hotel forty years ago.

But it had been the Oliver family's long-established feud with the Carlucci family, dating back to a time in Chicago when both families had been involved in shadier business practices, that had sparked the idea for Kit's first novel. The Montagues and the Capulets had nothing on the Olivers and the Carluccis. And although both San Francisco families were legitimate now, they were still bitter rivals when it came to business.

There was another burst of static. "…To talk to you. My cell is 546-2122."

Even as he filed the number away in his mind, Kit rose and moved toward the phone. But the line had already gone dead when he picked it up. He stared thoughtfully at the receiver for a minute. Why would Sadie Oliver need to talk to him?

He was punching in her number when another voice grabbed his attention.

"Excuse me."

The hoarse sound had him whirling, and as he did, he stubbed his bare toe on the leg of a chair. Swearing softly, he grabbed his throbbing foot and stumbled against his desk. The phone and the answering machine crashed to the floor.

In the midst of the chaos, all Kit could do was stare. Straddling the threshold between his office and his secretary's was a beautiful waif who could have graced the pages of any P.I. novel, including his own.

Here she is. That was the only clear thought he had as the tingling at the back of his neck morphed into an electric current. The tingling he understood. He'd been expecting something all day and she was it. He also understood the tightening in his gut. He'd experienced it before—that instant sexual awareness of a woman. The sensation of the ground shifting under his feet? Now, that was tougher to explain. But, hey, this was San Francisco. It could be a tremor.

And then it finally registered. The suit she was wearing was stained with blood.

3

"I…MAYBE, I SHOULD…"

She was going to turn and run. Pure panic shot through him and brought Kit out of his daze. He didn't trust himself to take a step yet, but he managed to speak. "Don't go."

She glanced down at a card she was clutching in one hand, then at Ari. "That's a very big dog."

"He won't move unless he smells food on you." In which case, Ari would definitely leap on her and she was such a bit of a thing that he figured the dog might just topple her over. Worrying about that brought the rest of his thoughts into focus. "You don't have any on you, do you? Food, I mean?"

"No…but…" She glanced uncertainly down at the card again. "I think I might be in the wrong place. I'm looking for…"

"Me." She was what he'd been waiting for all day. He was absolutely sure about that. And he was pretty sure the blood on her suit wasn't hers since she'd evidently gotten here under her own steam. So the tiny blonde with the bottle-green eyes was a damsel in distress of the first order. Her heart-shaped face and that perfect mouth might have been carved on one of the cameos his aunt Cass kept in her jewel box.

She was poised for flight. And no wonder. His office

looked as though it had just been attacked by the same tornado that had carried Dorothy off to Oz. There was a dog the size of a small bear cub lounging on the floor, and he…well, he just wasn't presenting his best professional image.

"Why don't you come in?"

She took one step and then paused again as if to gauge the response of the dog. In one quick glance Kit cataloged details, taking in the bruise that darkened the otherwise perfect skin near her left temple and the silky-looking hair that fell in tousled layers to just beneath a stubborn-looking chin. Last, but not least, he noted the first-rate legs and the designer open-toed shoes. Her other features remained hidden behind the dress bag and tote she was holding on to for dear life.

Kit had an overpowering urge to go to her, to press his hand to the small of her back and guide her carefully to one of his two client chairs, but he sensed that the slightest move on his or Ari's part would make her bolt.

"How can I help you?" he asked in a calm voice as he settled his hip firmly on the edge of his desk.

"I'm not sure you can." Her voice was stronger now. While he'd been studying her, she'd glanced warily around the room, her gaze settling on Ari twice. She met his eyes, then frowned down at the card in her hand. "I'm looking for Mr. Kristophe Angelis."

"You've found him." Kit sent her what he hoped was his most charming smile. Of the three Angelis brothers, he'd inherited the dimples. Most of the time he could have done without them, but every so often, especially when women were involved, they served him well. "I go by Kit. Kit Angelis."

She transferred her frown from the card to him, and this time when he looked into those green eyes, he felt a little punch right in his solar plexus.

"Have we ever met before?" she asked.

"No." Kit was absolutely certain of that—in spite of the fact that what he was feeling bordered on recognition.

"It says on this card that you're a private investigator." Her tone held a note of accusation—as if the card were lying.

"I am," he explained, "during the days. On my free nights, I write crime fiction." As he gestured around the room, a breeze sent more papers scattering to the floor. "You've caught me in my writing mode."

"I'm interrupting, then." She didn't appear to be at all reassured by his explanation. If their positions had been reversed, Kit wasn't sure he would have been, either.

"Not at all." It wasn't a lie, really. She hadn't interrupted. He hadn't even gotten one word down. Something she saw on his face must have reassured her—perhaps the dimples had finally kicked in—because she took a few steps forward. Good, he thought as he willed her to take a few more. He sat perfectly still while she did. Experience had taught him that luring a woman wasn't a lot different than reeling in a fish. Patience and persistence usually paid off.

She was close enough now that he could reach out and touch her. Kit had to suppress a powerful urge to do just that. He wanted very much to trace his finger along her jawline, to find out if that porcelain-delicate skin was as cool as it looked. He thought not, but a good investigator always tested his theories.

"You do investigate crimes, then?"

"Hmm?" Kit reined his thoughts in from the little detour they'd taken.

"You investigate crimes, right?" She was studying his face very closely.

He finessed his wallet out of his pocket, flipped it open and handed it to her. "I've been licensed by the state of California to do just that. I'm even allowed to charge for my services."

She glanced down at the wallet, then back at him. "Could you find out if I've committed a crime?"

He noted that her knuckles had turned white on the strap of the tote. He wanted very much to take that hand in his, but he kept himself very still.

"Probably."

"How?" she asked.

"My brother Nik is a cop. If a crime has been committed and the police are involved, he would know. I also have friends at the newspaper and TV stations. What kind of a crime are we talking about?"

"I'm not sure. Maybe a robbery. Maybe worse. That's what I need you to find out."

He said nothing, but he noted the way her grip tightened on the dress bag and the tote.

She held out his wallet to him, and when he took it, his fingers brushed accidentally against hers. Well, perhaps not accidentally.

The effect of that casual touch shocked both of them. She snatched her hand back as if it had been burned. And he knew exactly how she felt. The brief contact had sent a little current of electricity zinging along his nerve endings, and the knowledge that she'd been affected, too, had desire twisting his stomach into a hot, hard knot.

"I—" She faltered as if she'd lost her train of thought. He'd better damn well gather his own or he was going to lose her. He could read it in her eyes. She was still thinking of bolting.

Suppressing panic, he summoned up a businesslike tone. "Why don't you sit down and tell me who you are and what happened?"

She pressed her lips together firmly, drew in a deep breath and met his eyes. Beneath that fragile-looking exterior was an inner strength that he couldn't help but admire. "Are you any good at what you do?"

Considering the first impression he must have made, Kit couldn't fault the skepticism in her tone. He sent her another smile, again putting his faith in the dimples. "I'm the best."

She studied him for one more moment, then nodded. "I want to hire you, then."

Relief streamed through him. "Fine." He'd made the decision to take her case the moment he'd set eyes on her. There wasn't a doubt in his mind that she spelled trouble. But he was Greek enough, curious enough, not to turn his back on what fate dropped smack in his path. The twenty pages would have to wait. So would his fishing trip with Theo and Nik, if necessary.

"To make it official, I'll need a retainer. Do you have a dollar?" he asked.

"You'll help me, then?"

"Yes." Kit tried to ignore the feeling that he was agreeing to a lot more than a case.

She let out the breath she was holding and, for one brief moment, he thought she might lose that iron grip she seemed to have on her control. His admiration for her shot up a few more notches when she didn't. Finally, she set the leather tote on a chair, opened it and dug out a twenty. "I don't have anything smaller."

Kit took the bill she offered and placed it next to his closed laptop. "Neither do I so I'll have to owe you nineteen." He met her eyes steadily. "Will you trust me?"

There was an instant of hesitation before she nodded. "Yes."

A careful lady, he thought as he smiled at her. This was a woman who preferred to test the waters before she jumped in. That wasn't his particular style, but he could admire it in others. "Good. Now, you said, "maybe worse." Can you be more specific?"

Drawing in another deep breath, she finally let go of the death grip she had on the dress bag and draped it carefully over the back of the chair.

Then she stepped to the side and pointed to the stains on her skirt. "It's blood, I think. I don't believe it's mine. I checked, and I'm not bleeding anywhere. But I don't know how it got there. I can't remember what happened."

"You can't remember?"

"I don't remember anything before the accident. I was in a taxi that was in a collision just a few blocks from here." She gestured at the bruise on her temple. "I must have bumped my head during the impact, and I don't remember anything before I came to in the backseat. I don't know my name, what I do or what may have happened before I got in that taxi."

Kit glanced at the tote. "What about a wallet? Do you have some ID in that bag?"

She shook her head. "I checked. And I couldn't find my purse in the taxi. Everything's a blank. And…there's a wedding gown in the dress bag. I don't know why I'm carrying it around. I could be on my way to my wedding or running away from it. I don't remember."

There'd been a thread of panic building steadily in her voice, and Kit felt some of it move through him. In sympathy? He might have accepted that explanation if he hadn't tasted something bitter when she'd mentioned she might be on her way to her wedding.

"If I was getting married today, if I loved someone enough to…make that kind of commitment, wouldn't I remember that?"

He sure as hell hoped so, just as he hoped that particular scenario had no basis in reality. "Perhaps you couldn't make the commitment. Brides and grooms get the jitters. A lot of them have second thoughts." A scenario he much preferred in this case.

He reached for her left hand. The little current of electricity zinged through him again, but this time he didn't allow her to snatch her hand away. "You aren't wearing an engagement ring, and there's no sign that you've been wearing one. No indentation, no telltale white mark even though you have a slight tan. I'd say you're probably not the bride."

"Why would I have the wedding gown?"

"Could be you're a relative. A sister—or a member of the wedding party."

She curled her fingers around his. "Right. I hadn't thought…or maybe I'm a wedding planner. That might explain why I have the dress?"

"There you go." The relief Kit heard in her tone was all the more recognizable because it matched exactly what he was feeling. Which was ridiculous. He had to get a grip. He'd met this woman…what? Five minutes ago? Even setting his physical attraction to her aside, he'd never before met a female who'd drawn so many emotions out of him in so little time.

He'd taken her on as a client, Kit reminded himself. She was in trouble, and the least she deserved from him was some professionalism.

That was what his mind was telling him. Still, he didn't let go of her hand. He wanted to hold on to it. On to her.

She frowned suddenly. "That still doesn't explain the blood. Or the rest of it."

"The rest of it?"

Squaring her shoulders, she pulled her hand out of his and drew in a deep breath. "There's a gun and a lot of money in the leather tote. Maybe…" She paused to moisten her lips. "I can't help thinking that maybe I stole the money at gunpoint and shot someone. I could be more than a thief. I could be a killer."

4

"THAT'S A POSSIBILITY," he said.

The matter-of-fact way Kit Angelis made the statement surprised her. He didn't look shocked or even the least bit disturbed that he might have taken on a killer as a client. For some reason, his calm acceptance of that possibility eased her nerves. Just a bit.

There was no denying the fact that the man was having the strangest effect on her senses. When he'd first whirled around to face her, he'd looked so dangerous and beautiful at the same time. He'd reminded her of an angel—one of the dark ones who'd been booted out of paradise.

What he didn't look like was a P.I. In fact, her first thought had been that she'd interrupted him in the act of burglarizing the office. But he'd been barefoot. A thief would be wearing shoes, right? Still, she might have run for her life if she hadn't also felt something like recognition ripple through her. And a definite…pull.

When his fingers had brushed against hers, she'd felt the intensity of that touch right down to her toes. She'd blamed it on the fact that she must still be in shock…and told herself to get a grip. But a few seconds ago, when he'd taken her hand to examine her fingers, she hadn't been able to pull away. She hadn't wanted to.

"Have you touched the gun?"

She shifted her gaze to meet his. "Pardon?"

"Have you touched the gun since you regained consciousness in the taxi?"

She suppressed a shudder. "No."

"Why not?"

"Because—" She paused to consider the question. "Well, it might have prints on it. Or it might accidentally go off."

"Or you might have an instinctive fear of firearms. A lot of people do." He extended his hand. "Why don't you let me take a look at the gun?"

She picked up the tote and handed it to him, careful not to bring her hand in contact with his.

"See. You're not even touching it now. You're going to let me take it out of the bag."

After setting the tote on his desk, he fished a handkerchief out of his pocket and used it to extract the gun. Then he lifted the barrel to his nose and gave it a sniff. "It's a Magnum," he said. "And it's been recently fired."

She pressed a hand to the sudden queasiness in her stomach. She was not going to faint.

"That doesn't mean you fired it."

She met his eyes, and the steady way he was looking at her helped her keep control.

"There's a serial number to trace. If it's yours and you have a license, then we'll know your name." Kit rescued the phone from where he had knocked it to the floor earlier and punched in some numbers. "My brother, Nik, will probably be gone, but his partner will be there. Running the serial number will take some time, but it will give us something to go on."

Once again, the calm, steady way he spoke soothed her

nerves. Instead of allowing her imagination to run wild because the gun had been fired, she tried to focus on the conversation Kit was having on the phone.

He laughed at something the person on the other end of the line said, and she had the distinct impression that the cop he was talking to was a woman.

"Dinah, if you can put a rush on that, I'll buy you a drink at The Poseidon."

Definitely a woman.

He laughed again, and the sound of it tingled along her nerve endings.

"Okay, okay. A dinner in the new dining room."

Something hot tightened in her belly, and her eyes widened. She could not be feeling jealous because Kit Angelis had invited a cop to dinner, could she? That would mean she was attracted to him and she'd only just met him. What she was feeling had to be shock. Didn't it?

She studied him for a moment. Objectively speaking, he was very handsome. His face had the lean, strong features that ancient artists had liked to capture in marble and bronze. His nearly jet-black hair was on the long side and untamed. Standing there barefoot in threadbare jeans and a T-shirt, the man looked a bit untamed, too. And large. She felt something begin to pulse right in her center. He had broad shoulders, a narrow waist, long legs. And narrow feet. For some reason, she found his bare feet…sexy.

The pulsing in her center deepened. Okay. So maybe it wasn't merely shock. She *was* a bit attracted to him. It was a natural reaction on her part. The man would speed up the pulse of any woman who had one.

But it was definitely *not* jealousy she was feeling—just because he'd asked another woman out to dinner. That was ridiculous. She was in trouble. He was going to help her. The cop on the other end of the line could have dinner with him anytime she wanted. She wished both of them well.

Kit hung up the phone and shifted his gaze back to the Magnum. "You know, this is definitely not a lady's gun."

She couldn't have said why his comment had her lifting her chin. "Maybe I'm not a lady."

His grin was quick and charming. "Sugar, you're a lady right down to the tips of your toes."

Her eyes narrowed. "And you would know that because?"

His smile widened. "I'm a crack-shot investigator. I make a good part of my living noticing and cataloging the details. Look at your feet."

She glanced warily down at the open-toed shoes and blinked. Her toes were painted red.

"Those shoes, if I don't miss my guess, have a designer name on them. I'd say Italian. My kid sister, Philly, would give up lunches for a month to own a pair. I'm guessing the suit you're wearing has a designer label, too. Plus, you've got a pedicure. And a manicure."

She unclasped her hands and studied her nails. They were clean, neatly filed, painted with a clear polish except for the white tips.

"It's a special kind of manicure—with some kind of name. Philly told me once." Kit paused, narrowed his eyes and snapped his fingers. "French. It's a French manicure. And according to my sister, it costs extra. So you're certainly not trailer trash. You either come from money or you work hard to earn it. And you use some of it to take good care of yourself."

Was she the kind of woman who had nothing to do but

shop and go to beauty salons? Was getting a manicure and a pedicure the highlight of her week? She sincerely hoped not. She thought of the money in her tote. Maybe it belonged to her. Maybe she'd earned it. She much preferred the latter. But how had she earned that much money and all of it in cash? A thought popped into her mind. "Maybe, I'm a professional hit woman."

This time he didn't flash her that killer grin. Instead, he looked at her as if he were considering the possibility. Not good.

"That's one possibility. Let's test it." He opened another drawer, took out a gun and placed it on his desk. It wasn't the same kind as the one he'd taken from the tote, but it was large and just as deadly looking. "Pick it up."

She hesitated for only a moment. Then she lifted it with her right hand. It was heavier than she'd expected and she nearly dropped it.

"You're not holding it like a professional," he commented.

She shot him a narrow-eyed look. "I'm suffering from amnesia, remember?"

"If I asked you to boot up my laptop and search the Web for information on amnesia or memory loss, would you know what to do?"

She glanced at his computer and considered. "Yes. Yes, I would."

He smiled at her. "There you go. The gun isn't as familiar to you—therefore, you're probably not a professional hit woman. Why don't you try pulling the trigger? Aim it at the wall over there. It's not loaded."

More than anything she wanted to set the gun down on

the desk, but she didn't. Instead, she clasped it with both hands, raised it and pointed it at the outer wall of the office.

Even as she tightened her finger, her hands began to shake. A chill moved through her and, in spite of the heat in the room, she very nearly shivered.

She wanted to drop the gun and run. Biting her lower lip, she steadied her grip on the gun and squeezed the trigger. In the quiet room, the click sounded like a gunshot. Immediately, an image flashed into her mind—quick and bright as lightning. She was in a room filled with shadows. She was breathing hard as if she'd just run up a flight of stairs and there was a musty smell that was somehow familiar. Beneath that, she caught the scent of something else. Roses? A shadow shifted and a door in front of her opened slowly. Fear—an icy ball of it—lodged in her throat. Her hands shook. She couldn't steady them, but she was going to shoot—she had to—

When the dark figure slipped into the room, she pulled the trigger. And saw the figure stumble back into the wall. Deafened by the sound, blinded by the bright flash of fire, she stumbled backward herself and hit something hard. Hands gripped her upper arms.

"Easy, sugar. I'm right here."

Her head spun once, and then she remembered. Kit Angelis, the P.I. She'd hired him to help her.

"It's all right. Just take a deep breath and lean on me for a minute."

She did. But even as her vision cleared, she felt her whole body begin to throb. He continued to talk to her in that calm, steady tone, but she couldn't make out the words. Her senses were so filled with him—his body was rock hard at her back and so were his hands. She could feel the press of each one of his fingers through the fabric of the suit on her upper arms. Her mind suddenly filled with the sensations of what those fingers would feel like moving over her bare skin—over her throat, her breasts, her waist, and lower…lower. Oh, she knew exactly where she wanted those fingers to press.

"Take another breath."

She breathed in, trying desperately to rein in her unruly thoughts.

"You remembered something."

His words brought the memory back clear as crystal. How could it have slipped away—even for a moment? "I shot someone."

He turned her then and, after settling her in a chair, knelt down in front of her.

"Who?"

He wasn't touching her now. Instead of feeling…bereft, she should be grateful. The man was trying to help her and she wanted to just…jump him. What was wrong with her? She couldn't blame this on shock. It had to be something else.

"Close your eyes. Try to picture it like a video."

He was trying to do his job, trying to help her. The least she could do was help him. She took a deep breath, closed her eyes and tried to recapture the image of the shadowy figure opening the door and slipping into the room. "I can't make out his features. The room was so dark."

"Him?"

She thought for a moment and then nodded. "Yes. The figure was large. Tall and broad. I'm positive it was a man."

"Did you see him fall?"

She shook her head. "He stumbled backward into a wall, and I can't remember what happened next."

"What do you recall about the room?"

She frowned. "Nothing—no wait—there was a musty smell…the scent of old books. And—" her heart skipped a beat "—I smelled flowers, too. The bridal bouquet?"

Panic sprinted through her. She wasn't sure how, but her fingers were laced with Kit's when she opened her eyes. "What if I'm not the bride or the sister or the maid of honor or even the wedding planner? What if I'm a jealous ex-lover of the groom and I shot him for revenge? Maybe I shot the bride, too."

"Whoa! As a writer, I'd like to steal that idea for a plot. But as a P.I., I prefer to stick to the facts. The jealous, revenge-seeking ex-lover scenario doesn't explain why you'd run off with the wedding dress. Nor does it account for the loot you're carrying around. Plus, all you remember so far is that you shot someone."

"Maybe I killed him."

"And maybe not. You saw him stumble backward. You didn't see him fall. Let's stick with that until we know more."

She stared at him. He was being kind, trying to reassure her. She wanted desperately to believe him, but her gut instinct was telling her that she'd shot and killed someone.

"Have you ever had to shoot anyone?" she asked.

Kit's gaze was steady. "Not yet."

But he could, she thought. She could see it in his eyes. If he had to, he could shoot someone. So could she. Did that make them alike? That strange feeling of recognition moved through her again. This was a man she wouldn't have thought she'd have anything in common with, but it seemed she did. Right now she wanted nothing more than to just lean into him, to put her head on his shoulder and ask him to put his arms around her.

Even as she tried to clear the image out of her mind, she was suddenly aware of just how close they were, of how still the room had become. His face was only inches from hers and she could hear each individual breath he drew in and let out. She could smell him, too—a combination of soap and something else that was dark and male.

His mouth was so close, but it was his eyes she was most aware of—she couldn't seem to drag her gaze away from them. Something about the way he was looking at her had changed. As his fingers tensed on hers, heat streamed through her and she saw the reflection of that heat in his eyes.

Right now, she saw in them the same hunger she was feeling. She wanted to kiss him, and he wanted to kiss her, too. All either of them had to do was to lean just a bit closer... She'd barely moved when the memory of that dark shadowy room once more flashed through her mind, and she jerked back. "I need to…we need to…"

He released her hands, but his eyes remained on hers. "Yes, we do."

There was a promise in his tone that had a little thrill moving through her. But as he rose and helped her to her feet, his voice became businesslike.

"It's a very good sign that you're having flashes of memory," he said as he moved behind his desk. "It prob-ably won't be long until you remember everything."

She drew in a breath and let it out. Her skin felt cold now that he'd moved away. It shocked her that she still wanted to kiss him. A total stranger. A man who could make her blood turn into hot lava with a look or the most casual touch.

What could he do when he really touched her the way she'd imagined only moments ago? When he touched her all over? *When* and not *if?* What was the matter with her? Was she sex-starved? She barely kept from dropping her head into her hands. She could not go on this way. She had problems here. Big ones. She didn't know who she was or exactly what she'd done. Throwing herself at the man she'd hired to find out just how bad her situation was— well, that was a sure path to disaster. She had to get a grip, keep her mind on business.

Kit was certainly doing that. While she'd been fighting off a lust attack, he'd been emptying the tote. The packets of bills were neatly aligned along the edge of the desk, and he was carefully thumbing through one of them.

Obviously, what he'd felt a few moments ago hadn't been as intense as what she'd felt. She drew in a deep breath and let it out. Maybe she'd hired the wrong man for the job. She didn't think she'd be having this problem if he were short, fat and balding. Her eyes shifted to the twenty-dollar bill he'd laid on the desk. She could take the retainer back and just tell him that she'd changed her mind.

She considered that option as she watched him count the money. He certainly was focused. And thorough. And perceptive. So far, he'd told her things about herself that she might not have noticed—at least, not for a while. Not to mention the fact that Kit Angelis didn't look at all shocked by the gun, the money or the bloodstains. He hadn't batted an eye at the memory she'd shared with him, either. Plus, she needed someone's help.

Just thinking about gathering up the wedding dress, the money and the gun and starting over with someone else was exhausting her. She glanced at the business card she'd set down on the desk when she'd picked up his gun. Someone had given her that card. Someone had sent her here. Fate? She didn't know if she believed in fate or not, but she wanted very much to believe that she was the kind of woman who stayed the course.

Kit set the last bundle of bills on the desk, then sat down in his chair and smiled at her. "Have you decided whether or not to fire me, yet?"

5

STARTLED, SHE SAID, "How did you—" Her eyes narrowed. "Don't tell me you're some kind of psychic?"

Kit managed not to wince when she said the word as if it were some kind of disease. But the way she was looking at him now was a great deal safer than the way she'd looked at him a few moments ago. Safer for him. She'd been pale as a ghost and, for a moment, all he could think of was kissing her. She was a client, but reminding himself of that wasn't doing a bit of good.

"Well, are you?" she asked.

"No. My aunt Cass would argue that my brothers and I have some latent psychic abilities that we've inherited from my mother's side of the family, but my sister, Philly, is the only one who really has a true gift."

Now she was staring at him as if he was a smear some lab tech was about to shove under a microscope. In pure self-defense, he summoned up the dimples. "Sugar, I don't have to be a psychic to read what you're thinking. You have the most expressive face and eyes I've ever seen."

At her skeptical glance, he continued. "For example, a few minutes ago you wanted me to kiss you. Then you started to worry about that. You glanced more than once at that twenty-dollar bill." He raised his hands, palms out.

"My conclusion—you're having second thoughts about hiring me. No psychic powers required."

He saw the flash of temper in her eyes. "Well, if I'm so transparent, then you already know whether I've decided to fire you or not."

"Touché." As he threw back his head and laughed, Kit had the satisfaction of seeing the corners of her mouth twitch. He hadn't seen her smile yet, and he wanted to. Very much. He wanted other things from her, too. If she hadn't pulled back from him, he would have kissed her a few minutes ago. He'd very nearly kissed her even after she'd pulled away, but he wasn't sure he could have stopped with just a taste of her.

Truth be told, the strength of his attraction to her made him nervous. And cautious. Women had made him cautious before. But nervous? Never. A smart man would keep their relationship strictly business for the time being. Kit had always thought of himself as a smart man.

"Since you haven't taken your retainer back, I'll give you my first report. Usually, I type them up, but under the circumstances, I'll deliver it verbally—if that's all right?"

"That will be fine."

She was sitting there with her hands folded on her lap, as prim as a nun. But there were passions simmering beneath that cool exterior. Kit reined his thoughts in and focused on what he'd deduced so far.

"Counting the twenty you gave me for a retainer, there's a cool twenty thousand here." He gestured toward the stacks of bills.

Her already straight spine stiffened. "Not a bad payoff for a hit of some kind."

"Based on the way you handled my gun, I still don't think you're a professional killer."

"I did shoot someone."

He met her eyes steadily. "You might have acted in self-defense. And there are other possible scenarios. Perhaps you interrupted a hit."

She blinked. "I never thought about that."

He watched her consider that possibility, and he knew the minute that the headache hit her. Opening a drawer, he grabbed aspirin and a bottle of water and pushed them across the desk.

She shot him an accusing look as she reached for both.

Kit raised both hands, palms out. "Hey, you winced and your knuckles turned white. I'm a P.I. I make my living observing the details. And for what it's worth—I don't think you can force the memories. They'll come when you're ready."

"You know something about memory loss, then?" she asked.

"I had to do some research for the last book I wrote." Enough to know that it probably wasn't merely the bump on her head that had triggered her amnesia. "But I'm no expert." His glance dropped to the stains on her suit. Something had happened, something of a traumatic nature and she'd shot someone. That was what her mind was blocking. At least, that was the way he would have written it.

"Could I see your research?"

"Sure." Then he shot a rueful glance around the office. "It might take me a while to locate it. In the meantime, why don't you let me do my job? What we know for sure is that you've got a gun, no purse, a wedding dress, my business card and twenty thousand in cash. The serial number on the gun is being traced. You remember shooting at someone, you think it was a man. As a theory, we'll assume you hit him because of the bloodstains on your suit." He spread his hands on the desk. "That's what we know for sure. Agreed?"

"Yes. So what do we do now?"

He pulled a notebook out of a drawer and opened it to a fresh page. "I want you to start at the beginning and tell me everything you remember, everything that's happened since you regained consciousness in the taxi."

She'd gone tense on him again, he noted. "Try closing your eyes and picturing what happened."

"There isn't much to tell."

"Replay it in your mind like a video and don't leave anything out."

She did what he asked, and he jotted down notes in his own personal shorthand. For a while the sounds of traffic outside were muted by her voice and the movement of his pencil across the paper. When she finally finished, he set the pencil down and met her eyes.

"See?" she said. "There's nothing."

"On the contrary, I've learned a lot."

"What?" She leaned forward a bit.

"Number one, you're smart. In spite of everything that happened—the accident, the discovery that you couldn't remember anything and that you had bloodstains on your suit—you acted in a calm and logical way. You searched for clues. You asked the taxi driver the right questions. Number two, you told me the story in a clear, straightforward way, revealing that your mind works logically. Three, you're meticulous. If you recalled something, you went back and filled it in. And the way you described examining the dress bag and tote looking for clues tells me that you'd make a pretty good P.I."

For the first time since she'd walked into the office, her

lips curved in a full smile, and Kit felt his heart stutter. Swallowing hard, he continued, "Four, you have a very good eye for detail." The way she described her short, belligerent taxi driver and the tall, skinny man who'd crashed into them had made the two men come vividly alive in his head—the gypsy and the scarecrow. "I'd say you're some kind of an artist. A writer perhaps, or maybe a painter."

She considered that, then said, "You're being very kind. You've left out number five—I'm a coward. When I heard the siren, my first instinct was to run from the cops."

"You're not a coward. You're cautious. You didn't merely run away. You came here and hired me to find out what happened. I call that smart and brave."

On impulse, he rose, circled the desk and held out his hand. "Come with me."

"Where?"

"You said you trusted me, remember?"

She put her hand in his and he drew her to the door that opened into a small bathroom. Gripping her shoulders, he turned her toward the mirror over the sink.

"What do you see?"

She looked intently at the image of herself. He saw hope bloom and then fade in her eyes. "I see a stranger."

"Look harder."

Her chin lifted. "Okay. I see a woman—blond hair, green eyes. Short, about five…"

"I'd say five foot two."

"She has pale skin, and she looks…scared and…fragile."

"At first glance. But look at that chin."

A tiny line appeared on her forehead as she studied her reflection. Then he saw a smile flicker at the corners of her mouth. "Okay. Maybe not so fragile."

"Does the woman in the mirror look like a cold-blooded murderer to you?" Kit asked.

"No. But…"

"But there could be circumstances under which she might fire a gun. I promise you two things—we'll find out those circumstances and we'll find out who you are. Okay?"

"Okay." Her eyes met his in the mirror then, and Kit felt as if he'd been punched right in the gut. Too late, the warning bells rang in his mind, telling him it was a mistake to have brought her in here—an even bigger mistake to have touched her again. But even as those thoughts appeared, they vanished from his mind in favor of more tempting ones.

He pictured the two of them, limbs tangled, in a dark room on a narrow bed. He pictured them right here in the bathroom, her skirt pushed up, her legs wrapped around him. Desire—that he could understand and accept. But in the past, it had always been simple, never this urgent. And the pressure, the tiny ache around his heart—he'd never experienced anything like it before.

Her eyes had darkened, her lips had parted. He could see the pulse beating frantically at her throat. If he turned her around and kissed her, she wouldn't resist. Perhaps if he had a taste of her, maybe if he felt that slender body pressed against his, just once, it would quench the fierce hunger growing in him.

And pigs fly, said a little voice at the back of his mind. But his body paid no attention to that voice. His hand was already sliding over her shoulder to her throat, where he'd imagined touching her earlier. Her skin was warmer than porcelain, soft as sin and so delicate that he could feel her pulse against his fingers. Desire sharpened into an ache. One taste. He had to have one.

Her eyes were still on his in the mirror when he said, "One kiss."

"Yes."

Kit turned her around and, before another thought could intrude, he pulled her up on her tiptoes and covered her mouth with his. The moment he did, he felt as if he'd ignited an explosive fuse. Sensations poured through him. He'd known she'd taste sweet—but her flavor reminded him of melting ice cream on a hot summer day. The kind you have to lick fast and hard. He'd thought he knew what that slender body would feel like pressed against his. But she was stronger and even more responsive than he'd imagined. He'd sensed the simmering passion beneath that cool, rather prim exterior. But actually experiencing it was undermining his already thin grip on his self-control.

He'd never been so aware of a woman before—the press of her nails through the thin cotton of his T-shirt, the quick catch of her breath when he nipped on her bottom lip, the soft press of her breasts against his chest. He wanted more.

It would be so easy to drop his hands down to her waist—to lift her onto the narrow counter and shove her skirt up. Whatever she was wearing beneath the suit, it wouldn't prove much of a barrier. Before either of them could think, he could be inside of her. And that's where he wanted to be. Inside of her. That's where he needed to be.

As need clawed through him, Kit dragged himself free and took a quick step back. They were both breathing hard, and it wouldn't have surprised him a bit if the expression on his face was as dazed as the one on hers. No one had ever made him feel like this. So desperate, so unsure of his control. So absolutely wonderful.

"What are we going to do about this?" she asked.

If grinning hadn't been beyond his present capabilities, he was sure he would have. "I think we both know the answer to that. But unless you want it to happen right now, right here, we're getting out of the bathroom." Since he didn't trust himself to touch her anywhere else, he placed his hand on the small of her back and urged her toward the client chairs. Then he circled behind his desk, putting it between them.

"We can't—" she glanced back at the bathroom, then at him "—we can't do that again."

Now he did grin. "The one thing I can be certain of is that we're going to kiss again. And more."

"But it's…crazy."

"I agree."

"We don't even know each other. We don't know who I am."

"I'm with you there, too."

She began to pace. "I don't know if I feel this way about every man I meet. Or if it's just you."

He didn't like the idea of her kissing other men any more than he'd liked the idea of her being a bride. "No one else has ever made me feel quite this way."

"Oh."

Yes—oh, thought Kit as he watched her return to the chair and sink into it.

"Then, surely, you'll agree we can't kiss again. At least, until you know that I'm not a killer or a thief."

Because he wanted very much to go to her, he leaned back in his chair. "Sugar, I can't give you any guarantees on that one. Number one, I don't believe you're either a killer or a thief. And I'm not sure it would make any difference if you were Lizzie Borden. I wanted to kiss you from the moment you walked in the office. And I still want to kiss you. I want to make love to you very slowly in a cool, dark room on a big soft bed."

She didn't say anything, but what he saw in her eyes made it almost impossible for him to stay seated behind his desk. *This is not helping. Stick to business, Kit.* "However, you are a client. And you're paying me to help you. You have a right to complain if I don't do that. So, for now, we'll stick to that. How does that sound?"

She met his eyes and nodded.

"Good." Picking up his pencil, he tapped it on his notepad and forced himself to focus. "In any case, it always comes back to the evidence. You walked in here with the wedding dress, a gun, the money and my card." He reached for it and studied it. "I wonder where and how you came by it."

"I don't know."

"Since I don't leave these lying around town, someone had to give it to you. Perhaps a satisfied client. I do have a few of those. I could go through my files, toss out some names and see if anything clicks for you. But first let's try this." Reaching into his bottom drawer, he pulled out a phone book and began to leaf through it.

"You're not going to just read off names from that, are you?"

Kit shot her a grin. "Have some faith. The taxi driver said he picked you up on Bellevue. You're carrying a wedding dress in that bag, so I'm going to check for churches on that street."

Her eyes brightened as she rose and came around the desk to peer over his shoulder. "I hadn't thought of doing that."

"That's why you're paying me the big bucks, sugar." He

flipped to the Yellow Pages and they began to scan the church listings together. They might have found it sooner if she hadn't laid a hand on his shoulder and leaned just a little closer. Though her palm rested only lightly on him, heat radiated from that contact point.

He caught her scent just as he eliminated St. Alban's Church. She smelled fresh like soap and water, and a man would have to get close to learn that. He was just past the Church of Latter Day Saints and moving on to St. Patrick's when she reached around him and began to trace one finger down the column. Her arm brushed against his, and his gaze shifted to her hand. It was delicate-looking, the fingers long and slender. Perfect French manicure aside, her nails were short. She worked with her hands. He'd lay odds on it. And he wondered—no, he had to know what they would feel like moving over his skin.

Focus, he reminded himself. And he might have if he could have stopped breathing—or if she hadn't chosen that moment to lean just a little bit closer. So close that if they both turned at the same time, his mouth would brush hers. The image filled his mind and he could no longer see the words on the page.

"Move your hand," she said.

"Hmm?"

They turned at the same time, and their lips did indeed brush before each of them drew back a little. He didn't have to wonder if she'd felt the same flash of heat that he had. He could see it in the darkening of her eyes, her parted lips and her quickened breathing.

"You need to…move your hand."

He knew exactly where he wanted to move it, but he was a professional, Kit reminded himself. He reined his thoughts in from the little detour they were once more taking and glanced down to where her hand was nudging his.

"It's blocking half the page."

"Right." That was when he saw the bracelet, and it instantly cleared the sensual fog out of his brain. He hadn't noticed before, probably because it had been hidden beneath the sleeve of her suit. The bracelet was made of small, flat gold squares, four of which were engraved with letters. "What have we here?" Lifting her wrist, he spelled out the letters. "D-R-E-W. Drew." He met her eyes. "Odds are it's your name. Does it ring a bell?"

She stared down at the letters and repeated the word, testing it on her tongue. "Drew." Something flickered in her mind. The sound of someone calling her that? "Drew, run! This way!" She tried to capture the memory, but it faded.

"You've remembered something else," Kit said.

"I think someone was calling me that, telling me to run. The name seems…familiar. I just don't— I can't be positive." She glanced down at the bracelet. If she remembered someone calling her that, and she was wearing a bracelet with that name engraved on it…logic told her that the name was hers. "Drew," she said again. For a moment, as the word lingered in the air, she allowed herself to hope. Shouldn't the simple sound bring more memories flooding back?

Seconds ticked by. Her hope dwindled.

"Nothing," she finally said. "Nothing."

"You're wrong." He was still holding her wrist, and with his free hand, he tipped her chin so that she had to meet his eyes. "It's definitely something. I'm betting it's your name. So that's a start. From now on, that's what I'll call you, and you start to think of yourself as Drew.

Soon you'll have more. It's all going to come back to you, Drew."

There was something in the intent way he looked at her, in the sound of the name, her name, when he said it that made her want to believe him—to believe that he could make it all happen.

But it wasn't merely his kindness that she wanted. She wanted more than anything else to kiss him again. When his lips had brushed against hers a moment ago, she'd felt the explosion of warmth right down to her toes. And it hadn't been fair of him to plant that image of the dark room with the big soft bed in her mind. Hadn't she decided that she would have to be the strong one? How could she kiss him again? How could she even let herself think of what it might be like to make love with him when she didn't know anything about herself?

But she couldn't think of anything else. Right now, all that seemed to matter was how fast the pulse at her wrist was racing against his thumb. Her heart was racing, too. And his mouth was so close.

She should move, pull away, but she'd lost the will to do so. He moved a finger over her bottom lip and she trembled.

"You're so responsive. Watching you, I can't stop thinking of what it will be like to be inside of you."

"I…" Her mouth had suddenly gone so dry that words were sticking. Just as well, because what she wanted to tell him was that their thoughts were identical.

Her gaze dropped to his mouth and, for a moment, neither one spoke or moved. She wasn't sure she could do either. She realized that he was leaving it up to her. There was a sweetness to him—an irresistible contrast to the danger she'd sensed in him from the beginning. A smart woman would draw back. And hadn't he said she was a smart woman? Plus, she was logical. But there was nothing logical about what she was feeling—it was purely sensual. But he'd also said she was an artist. And they took risks, didn't they?

She wasn't sure quite how it had happened, but suddenly he was closer, his mouth just a breath away from hers. She wondered if she'd ever wanted anyone quite as much as she wanted Kit Angelis right now. Throwing caution to the wind, she pressed her mouth to his.

The moment she did, he took over the kiss, moving his mouth expertly over hers, parting her lips with his tongue. Yes, she thought. More. Whatever her reservations, there was absolutely nothing not to like about kissing Kit Angelis. Pleasure moved through her from each and every contact point—the press of his mouth, the scrape of his teeth, the arousing slide of his tongue. And there was such heat—glorious waves of it crashing through her until she was sure her bones were disintegrating. Tension, fear, all of her worries evaporated until she was aware of only this moment, this man.

Had anyone ever made her feel with such intensity before? If they had, surely, she wouldn't have forgotten. One of his hands cupped the back of her neck, the other gripped her waist, but she felt as if he were touching her everywhere. She couldn't wait until he actually did.

When he drew back, they were both breathing hard.

"Don't stop," she said.

"I won't." He moved a thumb over her bottom lip. "I can't."

"Neither can I."

This time it was Kit who closed the distance between them and pressed his mouth once more to hers.

Here she is. Here she is. The words thrummed in his blood as her taste once more poured through him. The sweetness was still there, but beneath it was the darker nuance of a desire as desperate as his own. Dragging his mouth from hers, he sampled the skin at her throat. It was damp, salty and vibrating with the sound of his name.

His name. The sound of it on her lips sent an avalanche of feelings ripping through Kit. Needs sharpened to an ache in his center. He couldn't get enough of her. He might never get enough. Hadn't he known this would happen? Hadn't he foreseen that she could strip him of control?

Even as the questions formed in his mind, her fingers dug into his shoulder and she wiggled on his lap trying to straddle him. Minds in tune, he lifted her off him and their fingers tangled, fumbled, as they sent her skirt sliding to the floor. The breath backed up in his lungs as he stared at the tiny scrap of white lace she wore beneath.

"Wait." She would have climbed back onto his lap if he hadn't pressed the palm of one hand flat against her stomach, trapping her between the chair he sat in and the desk. The soft dampness of her skin nearly distracted him, but he couldn't take his eyes off the thong. "I wondered what you were wearing under that skirt."

He drew one finger of his other hand along the satin ribbon hugging her hip and then slowly down the triangle of lace to where it disappeared between her legs.

He fastened his gaze on her and watched those sea-green eyes darken and then glaze as he pushed aside the lace and eased two fingers into her. Wet heat enfolded him.

"Kit!"

She was so hot, so ready, but he kept his eyes on hers. "Do you want me to stop?"

"No. Please."

He shifted the hand that he held pressed against her stomach, easing his thumb beneath the lace triangle until he found the little nub of her desire. He rubbed it hard as he pushed the two fingers of his other hand into her again.

She cried out his name again as her hips arched forward, and his control nearly snapped. But he wanted…no, he needed to give them both more. Gripping her hips, he settled her on the edge of the desk, then pushed her legs apart, knelt down on the floor and began to use his mouth on her.

She felt as if she were stretched on a rack trapped between pleasure and torture. Pleasure—waves of it—washed over her and through her as his tongue licked the wet heat at her center. But the pressure wasn't hard enough. He didn't go deep enough. And his hard strong hands held her thighs in a firm grip so that she couldn't move. Her own gripped the edge of the desk, struggling to hold herself upright as the tension inside of her built to the breaking point. But at the last moment, he drew away and trailed kisses down one thigh and then the other. The scrape of his teeth, the rough texture of his tongue, sent twin sensations of fire and ice along her nerve endings.

When he came back to where she wanted him, she could only feel his breath—teasing, taunting, until the ache inside of her grew sharp.

"Kit! Please."

As if he'd been waiting for just that signal, he pressed his mouth fully to her center and used his teeth and tongue. Heat scorched through her, as his thumb rubbed her clitoris and his tongue stroked into her over and over again. The climax built quickly, erupting and ripping through her in one wave after another.

Afterward, she lay on the desk, watching him through slitted eyes as he pushed down his jeans and sheathed himself in a condom. She couldn't move, could merely look on as he raised her legs, resting them on his shoulders and gripped her hips, drawing her forward.

She hadn't thought she could feel more, but the moment she felt those hard hands grip her hips, heat scorched through her again. When he thrust into her, she was instantly tossed back into a world of sensations. Her skin burned where his fingers dug into her hips. Her breath backed up in her lungs. And his eyes…the way he had of looking at her intensified the pleasure of each thrust.

Vaguely, she was aware that a phone rang. But it was only a distant noise. All she could focus on was Kit and what they were doing together. As he began to move faster, she moved, too, arching upward to meet his thrusts, using her muscles to tighten around him each time he filled her.

"Drew," he murmured.

The name felt so right to her when he said it. "Do you want me to stop?"

"No. God, no."

She knew the moment that his climax began. She saw it in the tightening of his jaw and in the narrowing of his eyes.

"Come with me, Drew." His voice was a hoarse whisper as he began to thrust even harder, even faster.

And when she heard his cry of satisfaction, she did.

KIT HAD NO IDEA how he ended up on the floor with Drew on his lap. But that was where he found himself when his brain cells clicked back on again. Drew's head was snuggled into his shoulder. She was still wearing her thong—although it was slightly askew—and her suit jacket, fully buttoned. The combination was incredibly erotic, but he was not going to attack her again. Not yet.

And he was not going to let either of them regret what they'd just shared. He tightened his grip on her and brushed a kiss over her temple. "You okay?"

She lifted her head and wiggled off of his lap. "I'm fine." She reached for her skirt. "I think you got a phone call while we were—otherwise engaged."

"A phone call?"

She got up and walked around the corner of the desk.

"Where are you going?"

"Bathroom," she said. "And I'm right. You did get a phone call. The message light is blinking."

By the time Kit made it to his feet, the bathroom door was closed and the message light on his phone was indeed blinking. He hadn't heard it ring—but she had. He'd have to think about that later.

After they talked. He knew by her behavior that they would have to talk about what had just happened. He wasn't having any regrets, but she sure looked like she might be having some. He pressed the button on his answering machine and fast-forwarded through his previous calls from Theo and Sadie Oliver.

"Hey, bro."

He recognized Nik's voice at once.

"You're probably already on your way to join Theo at the cabin. I might not make it. Something's happened. I'm at St. Peter's Church and there's been…well, I'm not sure yet what's going on. But the evidence is pointing to an

interrupted wedding even though there's no sign of the
bride or the groom."

Drew came out of the bathroom to stare at the phone.
"An interrupted wedding?"

"Look," Nik was saying, "the reason I'm calling is that
your friend Roman Oliver has been hurt. When I got here,
he was unconscious. It looked as though he'd taken a bad
fall down a flight of stairs. I'm not sure how serious his
injuries are."

Kit's stomach took a tumble.

"There's evidence that he was involved somehow in
whatever else went on here. I shouldn't be telling you this
much, but I thought you'd want to know. I'll call the cabin
and leave the same message with Theo in case you're en-
route. Roman's being taken to St. Jude's. Gotta go."

Kit stared at the phone, trying to take in the message.
An interrupted wedding and Roman was involved. And he
was hurt badly enough to be taken to the new trauma center
at St. Jude's. When he glanced up, Drew was leaning over
the phone book.

He knew what she was going to say the moment she
met his eyes.

"St. Peter's Church is on Skylar and Bellevue."

6

KIT PARKED HIS CAR in front of a fire hydrant half a block down from St. Peter's Church. He handed Drew the keys. "If a patrol car stops by, you can move it. But I doubt that any of them will be thinking of making their quota of parking tickets."

At least, not from the looks of the crowd that had congregated in front of the church. The press had obviously caught wind of the story. He turned back to her. "I'm depending on you to be a woman of your word, Drew."

She'd insisted on coming along. Her argument had been that if she went into the church, she might remember something. His argument had been that if she went into the church with bloodstains on her clothes, she might end up in jail.

Kit had long ago learned the only hope a man had of winning an argument with a woman was to present your most convincing evidence first. And then hope that the Fates were smiling on you. In this case, he'd conceded round one. She was here with him. But he'd won round two. She'd promised to stay in the car. Ari was presently sharing the backseat with the wedding dress and the tote. "If you get bored, you'll find some notebooks and pencils in the glove compartment. Practice writing your name. See if that jogs any memories loose."

"Go," she said, placing a hand on his arm. "You need to find out what happened to your friend."

He covered her hand with his. He'd told her about Roman on the drive over, and her words and the understanding in her eyes moved him. "I'll find out as much as I can, and I won't be long."

She nodded.

"Lock the doors and don't talk to strangers."

Her lips curved a bit at that, and Kit gave her a quick kiss. It took some effort, but he resisted the urge to deepen it. Instead, he got out of the car, shut the door and headed up the street. They still hadn't talked about what had happened between them in his office. He wasn't sure what he could say about it—except that it had been unlike anything he'd ever experienced before—and he intended to make love to her again, soon.

But he could sense that Drew might not be of the same mind that he was. Ever since she'd come out of the bathroom, he'd felt that she'd erected a little wall between them. One that he intended to go over or under or knock down. Later. Right now, he had to keep his mind on business. Professionalism was the key if he was going to help her. And he also needed to find out what had happened to Roman and how his friend was involved in all of this. All during the ride over, he'd tried his best to ignore the tingling at the back of his neck that was telling him what he was about to learn wouldn't be good.

As Kit crossed the street, he focused on details. Several TV news crews were stationed in front of the crime-scene tape at the bottom of the steps with cameras and lights at the ready. He recognized one of the uniforms as a friend he'd played basketball with in high school. Jerry would be his ticket in to see Nik. But, first, he was going to see what he could learn outside.

St. Peter's was an older church, one that had survived the earthquake of 1906. He'd read about it in the papers recently. Its new pastor, who preferred to be called Father Mike, had been profiled as a priest who'd taken an older inner-city parish and managed to revitalize it, making it a magnet for young people. Young people meant weddings and christenings, and according to the article, St. Peter's and Father Mike had been doing a thriving business recently.

A few feet away, Kit recognized the reporter who was in the middle of taping a live update for Channel Five. She was an attractive redhead named Carla Mitchell and she had a nose for news.

"All we know so far, Chet, is that two people have been taken away in ambulances to a local hospital. No word on their names or their conditions. The police aren't releasing any information until next of kin are notified."

Kit watched as Carla extended her time on the air by directing the cameraman to scan the front of the church. She filled her viewers in on the recent popularity of the church and speculated on whether or not this was a wedding gone tragically wrong. Kit's stomach tightened at the thought. There was very little doubt in his mind that this was the place where Drew had shot someone. But what in the hell had Roman been doing here?

The moment the camera stopped, he moved closer.

"Carla?"

"Kit."

He caught the recognition and brief flash of pleasure in her eyes before they narrowed in speculation. He and Carla had shared a few mutually enjoyable dates. They might have shared even more, but she was an ambitious young woman, and he was related to both a cop and an up-and-coming defense attorney. It hadn't taken Kit long to realize that she saw him a potential source of hot tips, and it hadn't taken Carla long to realize that he wasn't going to be providing any. They'd parted as friends.

She closed the distance between them and laid a hand on his arm. "Have you got a client here?"

He shook his head. "You're always on the job."

Carla grinned at him. "Always."

He turned on the full-dimpled smile. "I've got a brother here."

Her eyes brightened instantly. "Nik's here? You got any idea what the hell's going on?"

Kit shrugged and shoved his hands in his pockets. "No idea. I've got something personal I have to see Nik about."

"Right," she said.

"Really. It's family stuff. I just tracked him down."

"And pigs fly."

"So cynical." He glanced innocently around. "I really had no idea I was coming to a three-ring circus."

"Oh, it's that, all right. And there's a story here. I can smell it. I haven't gotten much but a few rumors so far. One is that shots were fired. A lady who lives down the block swears to it."

Kit didn't like the sound of that. "Any idea who they carried off to the hospital?"

Sighing, she shook her head. "Your brother runs a tight ship. Either the uniforms don't know anything, or they're afraid for their jobs."

Kit hid a smile. He was betting on the former. Nik had probably made sure that they had nothing useful to leak.

"Uh-oh," Carla said. "That's got to be the commissioner's limo pulling up. What did I tell you? Something big is up." She signaled to her cameraman and moved quickly toward the squad car and the limo that had pulled up to the corner. A few feet away, she turned back. "You find out anything from your brother that I can use, I'll make it worth your while."

And if he had continued dating Carla Mitchell, that would have been their relationship in a nutshell. Knowing that he'd have to work fast if he wanted a few private words with Nik, Kit strode toward his friend Jerry and seconds later, he was walking into the vestibule of St. Peter's.

He found his brother at the side of circular iron stairs that led to a choir loft. Nik was staring down at the taped outline of a body that was no longer there. The initial expression on Nik's face when he glanced up was fierce enough to have Kit nearly taking a step back. Shades of his childhood, he thought. Even as a kid, his oldest brother had been a formidable opponent. Though he was an inch or so shorter than Kit, Nik was built like a boxer. In a fight he was quick and mean—Aunt Cass claimed that he was the warrior of the family. Right now Nik definitely looked the part.

"What the hell are you doing here?"

Kit merely raised his eyebrows. "You left me a message about Roman, remember? What happened?"

"I can't talk about an ongoing investigation," Nik said. "Go away."

Kit had learned at an early age that Nik's bark was always worse than his bite. All it took was a little patience to wear him down. Through the open vestibule door, he could see a crime-scene cop at the altar taking pictures.

"You already called me and gave me information. You said that Roman had taken a fall and he was unconscious. How badly is he hurt? What happened to him?"

Nik sighed and shook his head. "I wish to hell I knew. He was unconscious when I found him. Either he was fighting with someone and his opponent shoved him, or they fell together. Either way, Roman definitely got the worst of it. I figure he went over the railing at the top and landed here. If he was fighting with someone, the other guy walked away."

Kit glanced up the stairs as Nik was talking. They were steep and circled up into the loft with nothing but an iron railing on one side. His stomach clenched as he pictured Roman standing at the top and being shoved backward over the railing. "What did the medics say?"

Nik met his eyes. "They were worried about a possible skull fracture or spinal injury. They won't know more until they get him to the hospital and take X rays."

The knot in his stomach tightened. "He's at St. Jude's Trauma Center, right?" It was the best place in the area, and the Oliver family had paid the full shot for it.

"Yeah, but you won't be able to get any information if you're not family."

Kit shot his brother a look. "I'll get the information." He returned his gaze to the staircase, and that was when he spotted the purse. It was in an evidence bag, clearly visible on one of the iron steps. Could it be Drew's?

His eyes returned to the taped outline. It took only that to have his mind flooding with memories—Theo playing tennis with Roman and losing; Roman and Nik racing sailboats at the fishing cabin; Roman swimming to shore with Philly holding on to his back on the day that he'd gone sailing with her and a sudden storm had come up. If Roman hadn't gone with Philly that day, odds were that the sea would have snatched another member of his family away from them. "He'll be all right," he finally said.

Nik placed a hand on Kit's shoulder.

Kit glanced back at the purse. "You mentioned an interrupted wedding in your message—and that the bride and groom are missing? Why was Roman here? I ran into Carla Mitchell outside. She has a neighbor who claims she heard shots."

Nik ran his hand through his hair. "I'm still trying to piece it together. I came in through the open door of the sacristy and found a dead body. Big bruiser of a guy with a Glock still in his hand. The priest—Father Mike—is on the altar, shot once in the shoulder. Bled quite a bit and he passed out. It's going to be a while before I'll be able to talk with him or Roman. My only witness who's conscious and able to talk is a caterer who claims there was a wedding going on. And she's a real pip. Says she was in the rectory dining room setting up the reception when she heard a quarrel—two male voices and one of them calls the other 'Roman.' Says, 'Roman, no!' Then shots are fired. Another male voice says, 'Get out of here. Now.' When the caterer hears hear the shots, she calls 9-1-1 and races into the sacristy to investigate."

He scowled. "She's lucky to be alive. She finds the body in the sacristy. Then she sees one of the shooters at the altar aiming a gun at Father Mike and she throws her cell phone at him. If she hadn't distracted him and spoiled his aim, the priest would probably be dead. She runs, manages to hide in a closet until I get here. At least she had enough brains to put a call in to 9-1-1."

"She saw *one* of the shooters? How many were there?"

Nik counted on his fingers. "The dead guy with the Glock is one. Caterer saw him arrive with the groom, figured him for a bodyguard. Roman's number two. His gun was fired. And there was the man at the altar who shot Father Mike."

A man, thought Kit. So it couldn't have been Drew. His stomach eased a bit. But his gaze once more shifted to the purse on the fifth step.

"There could have been more. I've got a man digging bullets out of the wall in the sacristy right now. And the caterer heard more shots after she ducked into the closet." Nik gestured up the staircase. "They were fired upstairs. There's a bullet hole in the wall and blood in this little room in the choir loft. There's also a bouquet of flowers. I figure the bride was up there. And she had a companion. The caterer says she saw the bride and another woman, a blonde, go in the back door of the church while she was unloading her van. But there's no sign of the mystery woman."

"What about the bride and the groom?"

"They're gone. I got a hell of a lot of people fleeing the scene of a crime."

"Sounds like the only ones who didn't were either shot, unconscious or hiding in a closet." Kit rubbed the back of his neck. He needed to get to the hospital to find out about Roman, but first, he had to see the upstairs room.

He said nothing. There was something that Nik hadn't told him yet. For a few minutes, he merely stood side by side with his brother looking down at the tape. He knew from experience that silences encouraged people to fill them. But the commissioner could finish with the press and walk through the door at any minute.

"You said in your message that Roman was involved in all of this. How? What aren't you telling me?"

Nik ran frustrated hands through his hair. "Off the record. You got that? The press is going to have a field day once they get hold of this."

"Off the record."

"The missing bride and groom—they're none other than Juliana Oliver and Paulo Carlucci."

Kit was so stunned that he wasn't able to speak for a minute. Juliana was Roman's and Sadie's baby sister, and Paulo was the only son of Angelo Carlucci, the head of the Carlucci family and business. His mind began to race. "They're just kids. Paulo can't be more than twenty. He just finished his second year of college. And Juliana's even younger—maybe eighteen or nineteen. It had to have been a secret wedding. Their parents couldn't have known...."

"Or they would have stopped it," Nik finished. "At least they would have tried to."

Kit agreed. "You think that's what happened here? Someone tried to stop the wedding and the plan went wrong?"

"Or the plan went right. The wedding sure as hell didn't take place."

The scene certainly fit that theory. The feud between the Olivers and the Carluccis hadn't lessened a whit just because their businesses had become legitimate. In fact, in the past few years, the rivalry had intensified. The families had no contact whatsoever. If the Olivers and the Carluccis happened to attend the same charity or political function, they kept their distances. A marriage between the two families would be viewed as a plot to infiltrate and uncover business secrets.

Kit knew exactly where Nik's mind was headed because

his had already leapt there. "You think Roman found out about the wedding and came here to stop it."

Nik met his brother's eyes steadily. "Could be. The evidence certainly supports that so far. And it could also be that Roman brought some firepower with him. Right now the best theory I've got is that Roman argues with Paulo Carlucci in the sacristy, shots are fired and the big guy, the bodyguard, is fatally injured. Paulo runs up to the choir loft to protect his bride. Roman follows. They struggle—more shots are fired. Roman falls or gets shoved down the stairs and the bride and groom get away."

Kit shook his head. "Roman has a temper. He wouldn't like the fact that his baby sister was marrying a Carlucci. But he would not come here to stop the wedding with a gun."

"Maybe not. But right now, he's the prime suspect. He brought a gun and he used it. I got a witness who heard him involved in an argument, and a fight broke out just before the first shots were fired."

"What about the man who shot Father Mike?"

"He could have been Roman's hired accomplice. So could the dead guy in the sacristy. Hell, there could have been more of them. There's blood on two different walls in that room upstairs. I'm betting the priest and the dead guy aren't the only ones who got shot."

Kit's stomach twisted. He had the mystery woman in his car less than a block away. At the very least, Drew could be a material witness. If that was her purse on the stairs as he suspected, they'd know her name and they'd be looking for her. But he didn't believe that she had any more to do with the shootings or disappearance of the bride and groom than Roman had. And with amnesia, she'd be very little help as a witness even if he turned her over to Nik.

Which he wasn't going to do. Not without consulting his client. "What about that purse?" he asked. "It doesn't belong to Roman."

"It belongs to Sadie Oliver," Nik said, his scowl deepening.

Kit said nothing. He didn't have time to feel relief that the purse didn't belong to Drew before his stomach took another long tumble. Sadie Oliver had been here? Then Nik voiced the suspicion that had slipped right into his own mind.

"Right now, it looks like Sadie came to help Roman stop the wedding. That's the way my captain and the commissioner are going to see it. And then she fled the scene of the crime—maybe with the bride and groom."

"Sadie Oliver called my office about half an hour before you did and left a message."

Nik's glance held surprise. "What did she say?"

"She said she needed advice. I was going to call her back, but I got distracted." Taking out his cell, he punched in the number that Sadie had given him. He looked at Nik as a ringing sound came from the purse. On the third ring, Kit disconnected the call.

"She must have called you from here, probably shortly after all of this went down," Nik said. "There was more than one call to 9-1-1. Maybe one of them came from Sadie. I'll check on it."

"There has to be an explanation," Kit insisted.

"I hope to God we find it," Nik murmured.

"Did you get in touch with Theo and let him know about this?"

Nik shook his head. "Theo isn't picking up his cell. You know how he is when he gets to that cabin. He wants to leave the city and business behind."

"He'll want to know about this," Kit said. "I have a feeling that Roman is going to need the counsel of a good defense attorney. If I have to, I'll go up there tomorrow and bring him back here. In the meantime, mind if I take a look at that room up there?"

Nik's eyes narrowed. "Of course, I mind. When has that ever stopped you once you set your mind on something?"

"Never." Kit bit back a smile. A brother knew you better than anyone. Plus, Nik had known Roman almost as long as he had. It hadn't been by chance that Roman had been transported to St. Jude's Trauma Center. Kit had a hunch that Nik had given explicit instructions to the EMTs.

With a scowl, Nik dug into his back pocket and brought out a pair of shoe covers. "The room's at the top of the stairs. Don't get in the way of my people and don't touch a thing."

"Thanks, bro. I'll be careful."

Just then, the front door of the church flew open behind Kit and a voice boomed. "There you are, Detective Angelis."

"Shit," Nik muttered under his breath. "It's the commissioner and my captain. There's a second staircase from the loft that leads to the sacristy. Use it when you leave."

Kit didn't have to be told twice.

7

DREW LOOKED THROUGH the window at the spot where Kit had disappeared. Though she'd been staring at that door for several minutes now, she couldn't find anything familiar about it. There was a part of her that wanted to believe this wasn't the place, that maybe she'd flagged the taxi on Bellevue near some other church.

"Dreamer," she muttered. This was the church, all right. She might not recognize it, but from the moment that Kit had parked the car, she'd felt a connection. It had been the same when she'd said the name on her bracelet out loud and she'd felt that flicker of memory that she couldn't quite bring fully to life. Her name was Drew. She was sure of it. And this church was where she'd gotten the bloodstains on her skirt. This church was where she'd shot someone with that gun.

This was also the church where Kit's friend had been seriously injured. Drew couldn't help but worry that Roman Oliver was the man she'd shot. The headache pounding behind her eyes grew more intense.

When she felt her nails digging into the palms of her hands, she concentrated on loosening her grip. Then she made herself take in a deep breath. Panic wasn't going to help.

In the backseat, Ari made a noise that sounded like a

yawn. She glanced down at her watch and saw that Kit had been gone almost ten minutes.

Of course, he'd spent the first four—not that she'd counted—talking to the redheaded and very attractive TV reporter. Drew couldn't help but notice the way the woman had smiled up at Kit and touched his arm in that intimate way. Though his back had been turned toward her, she'd had no problem picturing his answering smile. The man had killer dimples. No doubt about it. And it had been the attractive reporter who'd walked away. Not Kit. Her conclusion: the reporter and Kit had probably dated.

Probably? For all she knew, the reporter could be dating Kit now. They'd certainly looked like they were friendly enough. They'd probably still be chatting if that limo and squad car hadn't shown up.

Closing her eyes, Drew took another deep breath. She had a problem here. Over and above the fact that she'd shot a man and she'd lost her memory, she was, clearly, totally obsessed with Kit Angelis. She'd only known him for about thirty minutes when she'd thrown herself at him. She'd initiated that kiss and what had followed. He'd left it up to her and she'd…had sex with him. She'd had wonderful, explosive, mind-numbing, can't-wait-to-do-it-again sex with a man she'd never met before.

And a few minutes ago when he'd kissed her, just a light, friendly press of his lips to hers was all it had taken to stir up those edgy little needs in her again. It baffled her. It delighted her. He touched, she wanted. It was that simple, that primitive.

And when he came back to the car, she'd want to kiss him again. And more. Worse—she didn't seem to have any kind of defense against him. Not reason, not logic, not even the niggling worry that she might be some kind of nymphomaniac who wanted to make love to every man she met seemed to help.

Drew made herself look at the crime-scene tape, lights, reporters, uniformed officers and police cars, and reminded herself that she had bigger things to worry about than her irresistible attraction to Kit Angelis.

She had to at least try to get a grip. Besides, even if she wanted to have sex with Kit Angelis again—which she did—he didn't seem interested in repeating the experience. Ever since the phone message from his brother, he'd had been all business. He'd slipped back into his shoes and a lightweight jacket and he'd slipped his gun into the waistband of his jeans. More than anything else, that one simple action had snapped her back to reality. Not once on the ride to the church had he referred to what had happened between them. For him, making love on the desk in his office had probably been unremarkable.

In the backseat, Ari yawned again.

Drew shot him a look. "Exactly. He's probably done that kind of thing before. A 'ho-hum' experience. On a scale of one to five, maybe a three. After all, the only thing that makes me different from the other women he's made love to is that I might be wanted for murder."

She glanced back at the front door of the church. That couldn't be a turn-on. He was probably even now discovering things about her that would lead to her imminent arrest. The pounding at her temple picked up its rhythm.

In the backseat, Ari put some effort into sitting up. Drew glanced at her watch. Kit had been gone almost fifteen minutes. That couldn't be good. It had to mean he was learning things.

She should have gone with him.

Ari whined and placed a heavy paw on her shoulder. When she turned to look at him, she saw that he had the end of his leash in his mouth. He whined again.

"What?" But even as she spoke the question, she realized that he was probably asking to go out.

"Now?" she asked, recalling that Kit had made her promise to stay in the car.

Ari whined again, and she was sure she heard a note of desperation in the tone.

"Okay. Okay." She tucked the car keys into her pocket and pressed the button on the door that released all the locks. No sooner had she climbed out than Ari bounded to the pavement beside her. She'd never seen him move that fast, and she barely caught the end of the leash before he shot down the street.

Drew dug in her heels, but that barely slowed down their forward momentum. "Stop. We can't...whoa!"

What in the world had happened to the indolent animal who'd seemed permanently attached to the floor of Kit's office?

"Ari...please, stop!"

The dog ignored her, plummeting forward. When he reached the crime-scene tape that had been used to barricade the side street, he slipped right under it, forcing Drew to duck beneath it and follow. He halted when they arrived at the first of the parked squad cars. Luckily, the uniformed officers who belonged to it had moved to where a tall, distinguished-looking gentleman stood talking to the press by the limousine that had arrived earlier. Another man, younger but equally well dressed, stood next to him.

"We were supposed to stay by Kit's car," she blustered

to the dog. "Correction. We were supposed to stay in the car." Then she watched in horror as Ari moved directly into a pool of light that fell from a streetlamp, lifted his leg and took aim at the front tire of the squad car.

"Stop. Please. There's a perfectly good hydrant right next to Kit's car. You can't…"

Ari ignored her and continued his business.

She shot an apprehensive glance at the two uniforms, but they were still at the limo. A moment later, one of the officers escorted both men up the steps of the church. The news crews filmed the procession. At any minute the uniformed men could return to their car.

"Hurry," she urged Ari.

Seconds ticked away, and Drew felt like she was standing in a spotlight. Which she was. In her mind, she imagined the redheaded reporter Kit had chatted with rushing toward her, mike in hand.

When the dog finally lowered his leg, she let out a sigh of relief. "C'mon," she said, and tugged on the leash.

Once again Ari ignored her. Instead of moving back to the car, he stretched out on the pavement.

"Ari, please," she begged. "This is not the place for a nap." Out of the corner of her eye, Drew saw one of the policemen glance in her direction. When he started toward her, she squatted down and bent over, wrapping her arms around Ari so that the front of her suit was well-hidden. Her mind raced as she tried to think of an appropriate bribe for a dog. "When we get back to the car, I'll turn on the air-conditioning."

Ari didn't budge.

"Ma'am?"

Keeping a firm grip on the dog, she managed a smile for the cop. "Hi."

"I have to ask you to step back outside the tape. And take the dog with you."

"Working on it." Tightening her hold on Ari, she tried to heave him up off the pavement. It was like trying to move a boulder. "C'mon, boy."

In one surprisingly quick move, Ari rose, throwing her off balance. They both tumbled back and she ended up sitting on the pavement with Ari spread across her lap. Pleased with himself, the dog licked her face.

"I'm thinking of an obedience-training course," she said to the cop.

"Here, let me give you a hand." The officer started to bend over.

This was it. The knots in her stomach tightened. Once he pulled the dog off of her, there was no way to hide the bloodstains. She'd be in handcuffs, dragged away to jail.

"Food," she said.

The cop looked at her as if she were several cards short of a full deck. "Food?"

She shot him a smile. "He'll do anything for food. Tell me you've got some in your car. Doughnuts?"

He considered that for a minute.

"Please. I know you can probably handle him, but I don't want him to get hurt." That was such a lie that she wondered why her nose didn't grow as long as Pinocchio's. Truth be told, she wanted to strangle Ari.

He whined and licked her face.

The cop glanced at the dog, then at her. "I might have a doughnut. Just don't move until I get back."

There wasn't much chance of that, Drew thought as she watched the cop open the door of the squad car. Maybe if she weren't pinned to the ground by a large dog, she might have made a run for it. If Kit had any psychic powers at all, she prayed that they would kick in. Soon.

KIT STOOD in the doorway of the small room at one end of the choir loft. The loft was one of those that ran across both sides of the church as well as the back. The old storeroom was about eight by nine. One wall was lined with shelves where hymnals were stacked. They accounted for the musty smell that Drew had recalled. On the floor lay a wedding bouquet. The cops working the scene had already bagged it. There was no window. Without illumination from the overhead light, the room would have been very dark indeed. This was the room that Drew had recalled, all right.

A room where the bride and her companion had waited for the wedding ceremony to begin?

Kit glanced around again. Shots had definitely been fired in here. There was a bloodstain in one corner, and more on the wall near the door. There might well have been more than one victim. Recalling the details of Drew's sole memory, he imagined her standing in the corner to his right, pictured the door opening and a large figure moving into the room.

At that kind of close range, there was very little likelihood that she'd miss. So she hadn't shot Roman. But she'd shot someone. He saw the man entering the room, being hit by the bullet and then stumbling back against the wall. The scene worked.

The other bloodstain was on an outside wall, directly across from the door. If the man coming through the door had fired in that direction, he'd have hit his mark, too.

Had the man shot the bride? Or the groom? In his mind,

Kit tested the scenario that Nik had suggested. Following the argument in the sacristy, Paulo Carlucci ran up here to protect his bride. Roman followed, rushed in the door. And shot someone? Not his sister. Would he have shot Paulo? And if he was shot, how would Paulo have been able to overpower Roman and send him tumbling over the railing?

And who was the man Drew shot? Not Roman because he hadn't taken a bullet and Drew was certain she'd hit her target. So there must have been another man up here in this room. Unless Drew had shot the groom. Was she in on whatever had gone on here?

If he thought that, he would turn her over to Nik right now. But he didn't. He no more believed that Drew had come here to kill Paulo than he believed that Roman had. There had to have been another shooter involved. Someone who'd chased up here after Paulo. He considered Sadie in that role, then dismissed the thought. Drew had been sure she'd shot a man. So it had to be someone else, someone that Roman had come up here to deal with.

Kit ran through the scene again. The bad guy came into the room, fired a bullet at the bride or the groom and Drew shot the bad guy, who stumbled back into the wall and then out of the room. Roman struggled with the guy and took a header over the railing.

Kit liked that scene much better than the one Nik had described where Roman chased Paulo and possibly shot him. But so far he didn't have even a decent theory about why Drew had been packing a gun, let alone who the man she shot might have been. And what was Sadie Oliver doing during all of this? And how in hell did the money fit in?

Okay—he let his mind entertain Drew's theory that she was a hit woman. Then why come to see him with the money and the gun? And who had given her his card?

With a frown, Kit rubbed the back of his neck. Tingling sensation aside, a scenario with Drew as a hit woman just didn't ring true to him. She'd arrived with the bride. Perhaps she was the maid of honor. Maybe she'd used the gun to protect the bride.

Yeah, he liked that scenario a great deal more. And what part had Roman played in all of this? Roman had definitely been up here. He'd struggled with someone who'd pushed him down the stairs. And where in hell were the bride and groom now?

There was way too much he didn't know or couldn't explain.

One thing was for sure—his friend Roman was currently in big trouble. Drew wasn't out of the woods yet, either. And considering the explosive nature of the crime and the possibility that some members of the Carlucci and Oliver families might take the law into their own hands, the police were going to want to close the case fast.

The sound of footsteps climbing the staircase to the loft brought Kit's speculation to a dead stop. As quietly as he could, he left the room and strode toward the door at the far end of the loft. Slipping through it, he made his way quietly down the stairs and let himself into a small, dimly lit room that wasn't much bigger than a closet.

A woman let out a frightened yelp.

"Sorry." Kit turned in the direction of the noise and then simply stared. Handcuffed to the radiator she was presently perched on was a petite redhead in black pants, a neat white shirt and a black bow tie. A black ribbon had once probably held the tumble of red curls back from her face, but quite a number of them had escaped. Under other circumstances he might have described the face as pretty. Right now, it was furious.

"You're related to that…that…cop, aren't you?"

She managed to make the word *cop* sound like *bastard* or *son of a bitch*.

"Don't try to deny it. You've got the same eyes, the same drop-dead looks and the same cocky-as-hell attitude. Tell him if he doesn't release me right now, I'm going to have him brought up on charges of police brutality. And I mean it."

This had to be the caterer, Kit thought. And Nik had handcuffed her to a radiator? Interesting. Beyond her, he could see into a larger room where a crime-scene cop was snapping photos of a body on the floor. That had to be the "bruiser with the Glock" Nik had described to him. The one man who'd been shot and killed in the church that night. Returning his glance to the redhead, Kit flashed his dimples.

She waggled her finger at him. "Not going to work. He tried a smile, too. I may do more than have him brought up on charges. I may strangle him."

In spite of her warning, Kit kept his smile in place. "Just a piece of advice. I wouldn't say that in front of the other cops. They tend to take threats to their colleagues poorly. I'm Kit Angelis, Nik's brother. And you must be the caterer?"

"J. C. Riley."

"It's a pleasure, Ms. Riley. You mind telling me why Nik handcuffed you?"

She thought for a minute. When she finally spoke, Kit was sure he was getting the edited version. "Some mumbo jumbo about me being a material witness and he didn't want me bolting or mucking up his crime scene. As if I would. Seriously—" she rattled the handcuffs "—could you talk some sense into him?"

"I can try. But I'm his youngest brother. He doesn't pay much attention to me. I understand you saw Father Mike get shot."

Some of J.C.'s bravado faded. "Yes. And I saw the man who did it."

"Earlier you overheard an argument?"

She nodded. "I didn't catch the words, but Roman Oliver was involved in it. I heard the other guy call him by name. They were angry, and then the shooting began." She jerked her head toward the adjacent room. "They're digging bullets out of the wall right now."

"You heard more gunfire after Father Mike was shot, from up in the choir loft. Do you know who was up there? Or who else was invited to the wedding?"

She studied him for a minute. "Who are you—the good cop come in to grill me after I ticked off the bad cop?"

No wonder Nik had described her as a pip. She was definitely that. Kit raised both hands. "I'm not a cop. Roman Oliver is my best friend so I have a personal interest."

"Oh. I'm sorry. Is he all right? Your brother won't tell me anything."

"He's been taken to the hospital. Can you tell me who was invited to the wedding?"

"No. I never even met the bride or the groom. When Father Mike hired me, he said it would be just the wedding couple, the maid of honor, the best man and him. That's it."

"He mentioned a maid of honor and a best man?"

"Yes. I prepared a wedding cake and champagne for five, including Father Mike, of course."

"You can't make a lot of money on a small wedding like that."

"Father Mike recommends me all the time. So I take the small and the big. Good PR."

Instinct told him she was telling the truth. And a sudden intense tingling at the back of his neck told him that he'd better get back to Drew. "Nik says you saw a blonde come in with the bride." He thought of Sadie's purse. "You didn't by any chance see a tall brunette arrive?"

"No."

"Thanks. You've been a help."

"Hey!" J.C. called after him, "tell the bad cop to come back here and take these cuffs off."

"SORRY, I COULDN'T FIND any doughnuts, ma'am," the cop said.

"Me, too." Drew had somehow managed to get to her knees, and she was doing her best to help him budge Ari. The dog wasn't having it.

She had a lie all ready. She couldn't think why she hadn't come up with it sooner. She'd spilled a whole glass of wine on her suit. Surely he'd buy that. The only problem now was Ari. She shifted into a squat and tugged. "C'mon, boy."

"They're with me, Jerry."

At the sound of Kit's voice, the cop straightened and turned. Then Ari shot to his feet and barked a welcome. Drew felt her balance waver, then completely disintegrate. She would have toppled backward onto the pavement if Kit hadn't grasped her upper arms firmly. Then in one continuous movement, he shifted so that Jerry's view of the front of her suit was completely blocked.

"Did you find Nik?" Jerry asked.

"Yeah, thanks. He told me to make tracks once Commissioner Galvin and Captain Parker arrived."

"First time I've ever seen the commissioner come to a crime scene. Excuse me a minute." A van was approaching. Jerry ducked under the tape and waved the driver away. As soon as the van had done a three-point turn and headed back up the street, Jerry turned back and lowered his voice. "Nik give you any idea what went down in there?"

"No. I know about as much as you do." While he spoke, Kit lifted the crime tape, and Drew ducked her head to get under it. Once they were on the other side and out of the pool of light, Kit spoke to Jerry again. "As soon as Nik fills them in, I'm sure Captain Parker will brief all of you."

Drew waited until they had walked half a block and were out of hearing range before she spoke. "You must have found out *something*. You were in the church close to twenty minutes."

"I thought we agreed that you would stay in the car and let me do the investigating."

"I didn't have a choice. Ari had to relieve himself. And once I let him out, he dragged me to the nearest police car. What did you find out? Why is the commissioner here?"

Kit glanced down at the dog. "He dragged you to the nearest police car?"

"Yes. Then he lifted his leg and peed on it. Your friend Jerry didn't see him or he probably would have arrested me. And now that I've updated you on Ari's deplorable manners, will you please tell me what you found out."

Instead of looking apologetic about the dog's behavior or at least answering her questions, Kit grinned down at the dog. "Good boy."

Drew stopped short. "Good boy? You're praising him for peeing on a police car?"

Kit chuckled. "Roman and Theo and I trained him to do that when Nik was assigned to his first patrol car a few years back. It's good to know that Ari hasn't forgotten."

Drew's eyes narrowed. "The three of you trained him to pee on your brother's car."

"Yeah. He caught on real quick." Kit patted the dog's head.

She caught something in Kit's expression that had her reaching out to take his hand. "You found out something bad about your friend Roman, didn't you? How badly is he hurt?" Her earlier suspicion returned. "Is he the man I shot? Is he dead?"

"No." Kit met her eyes steadily. "Roman wasn't shot. He took a bad fall and he's at St. Jude's Trauma Center. I have to go there."

"Of course you do." Keeping his hand in hers, she quickened her step toward the car. Then ,because she wasn't sure what else to say, she asked, "Why did you train your dog to pee on your brother's car?"

"Older brothers can be a pain—they're bossy, arrogant. They think they know it all."

"And your friend Roman helped you with this project because…"

Kit's lips curved. "Probably because he was over at the house and restaurant so often that Nik had taken to bossing him, too. And as I recall, the three of us had had a few beers when the inspiration had struck." Lifting a hand to rub the back of his neck, Kit stopped to scan the street.

"What?" Drew asked.

"I just have a feeling…damn!"

"What is it?"

"That van up at the corner. It's the same one that Jerry just waved away from the church."

Following the direction of his gaze, Drew spotted the dark colored van parked near a Stop sign at an intersection about a hundred yards beyond Kit's car. For a moment, neither of them spoke, and in the brief span of silence, she caught the sound of a motor running.

"You think it's waiting for us?" Her stomach clenched.

"The tingling at the back of my neck is telling me it's waiting for *you*. And they've got us between a rock and a hard place," Kit mused. "If we go back to the church, the woman who was catering the wedding may recognize you. Hell, she may have already described you to Nik."

Drew momentarily forgot the van. "You did find something out. Whose wedding was it? Tell me."

"All in good time." Taking her arm, he urged her forward. "First, we're going to execute Plan A—which is to get the hell out of here. I don't think whoever's in that van will try to do anything here. There are a lot of cops around. But we're going to take it nice and easy, pretend we haven't noticed them. No point in making them panic."

"Try to do what?" She was the one about to panic. She could already feel her stomach jumping.

Kit must have sensed it because he said, "It's going to be all right. When I open the passenger door, we'll let Ari hop in first, then you'll get in and duck low."

Duck low. She didn't like the sound of that. "Why do I have to duck?"

"Just a precaution. The streets around the church are all blocked off, so the only way out of here is past that van. I don't think they'll try anything this close to those police cars, but…"

Drew didn't like the sound of the *but,* either. "The tingling at the back of your neck aside, why are you so sure whoever's in that van is after me?"

He shot her a grin. "Elementary, my dear Watson. *A*—because whoever is in it got a good look at you while they were turning back at the church, and they're hanging around. *B*—you've got twenty-thousand dollars in a leather tote. And *C*—whatever went down in that church, you were a witness."

Okay. Three good reasons why she had a perfectly legitimate right to panic. The jumping in her stomach accelerated.

"Maybe I should give myself up to the police."

"Nah." Kit continued to urge her toward his car. "You're not a coward."

"My stomach is singing a different song."

"I'll have to feed you." He squeezed her hand as they reached the front fender of the car. "Remember the plan?"

She nodded. "Ari, first. Then me and I duck low."

"Good girl." He turned her so that she was facing him and brushed his lips over hers. The contact was brief. She might have called it friendly except for the way his fingers tightened on her shoulders and the arrow of heat that shot through her and curled her toes. When he drew away, she felt so cool she nearly shivered.

"Let's go."

He opened the door, and she had to hand it to Kit Angelis. The plan went perfectly. Ari leapt into the backseat on cue, and she slid into the passenger seat, ducking her head low.

Seconds later, he got behind the wheel, buckled up, started the car and pulled away from the curb. Then he stopped, put the car in Reverse and began to back up along the street.

"We're moving past them," Kit said in a soft voice. Then he braked, changed gears and the car shot forward. "Now we'll see if my hunch was right."

She tightened her grip on the seat and reminded herself to breathe as the car accelerated.

"Brace yourself." Kit pulled the wheel hard and tires squealed as the car careened around a corner.

"What's happening?" She had to shout to be heard above the roar of the engine.

"Just what I was afraid of," Kit shouted back. "They're following us."

"What are we going to do?"

"Don't worry. I've got a plan."

8

KIT SAID A PRAYER under his breath as he ignored the Stop sign and shot the car straight through the next intersection. At the end of the street, he twisted the steering wheel and executed a sharp left turn. The car skidded sideways, nearly hitting a parked car before his tires gripped the pavement.

The Fates weren't working totally on his side yet. But they would. They had to. If he could just put some distance between his car and the van. He was about two blocks ahead of them. Aiming for three, he took the next corner on two wheels and prayed for more horsepower.

"Can I get up yet?" Drew asked.

"In a minute." Kit checked the rearview mirror and saw the van careen around the corner he'd just taken. "Okay, but get your seat belt on fast. We're not out of this yet." Not even close, he thought as he slammed the gas pedal to the floor. The engine roared. The speedometer barely wavered.

"Can't you get this car to go any faster?" Drew shouted. "I feel like I'm riding in the little engine that couldn't."

"Funny," Kit said, and barely suppressed a grin. "These hills are hell."

"They don't seem to be slowing down the van."

"I noticed." He caught a glimpse of Drew in his peripheral vision. She had her hands clasped tightly together in her lap, her knuckles white. She was scared to death, but she wasn't falling apart on him. "Don't worry, I've got a plan."

"So you said, but it doesn't seem to be working very well."

"Ouch." He wanted to laugh. Later, he would, he promised himself even as he wondered why that dry tone of hers got to him. "Hold on." The car crested the hill, went airborne for an instant, then slammed back onto terra firma.

"Hot damn! I've always wanted to do that," he shouted, then thanked the Fates when the speedometer finally began to climb. "Wheeeeeeeeeee!"

He was crazy. Why hadn't she noticed that sooner? Drew turned her gaze to study him because if she kept looking at the road, she was going to hurl up whatever she'd eaten for her last meal.

Last meal? That possibility was all too real—they could crash at any time, and she didn't even know what she'd eaten. All because she was riding in a car with a lunatic. If she could have dragged her hands away from the dashboard without losing her balance or the contents of her stomach, she might have hit him.

Did that mean she had a violent side? Well, of course she did. She'd shot someone, hadn't she?

Looking back at the street, Drew saw the traffic light ahead of them change from amber to red. She braced herself, but Kit merely laughed and ran the light.

How could she have missed this maniacal streak in the man? Initially, she'd thought him a dangerous thief. She'd been dead-on about the dangerous part, all right. It was there in his eyes right now as he gave her a quick glance.

But then, she'd bought his "I'm a part-time writer, part-time P.I." story. True, his explanation had seemed plausible. And he did love his dog. Plus, he was an incredible lover.

"Hold on!" he shouted. Glancing ahead, she had to bite back a scream. This time the light wasn't amber. It was pure red and they were rocketing toward it. Cars, fully confident that they had the right of way, streamed through the intersection at a fast clip. Even though she shut her eyes, she had a quick image of hitting one of them broadside. Then Kit was dragging the steering wheel to the right.

She was aware that the car almost went into a spin. Horns blasted, brakes shrieked. But the impact she was expecting didn't come. When she managed to open her eyes again, she saw that Kit had miraculously inserted the car into the right-hand lane of traffic, and they were moving at a much saner pace toward the next intersection.

To her surprise, Kit slowed for the amber and slid to a stop.

She turned to him and narrowed her eyes. "Why the sudden attack of caution?"

He glanced in the rearview mirror. "See the van three cars back?"

She turned and spotted it. "Yes."

"Eddie Murphy pulled this trick in *Beverly Hills Cop.* The first one. It's a classic."

The light turned green, and Kit didn't put his foot on the gas. Traffic in the lane to their left began to move through the intersection. Cars trapped directly behind them honked their horns. She even caught some interesting gestures in the sideview mirror.

"What are you doing? There's a green light."

"I'm just trying to put a little distance between us and that van. Keep your eye on it."

Behind, she saw a large vehicle trying to pull out into the left lane, which was moving fairly swiftly now. But there was too much traffic, too many frustrated drivers, and no one was letting them in.

"So far so good," she said.

The traffic light turned amber. The instant it turned red, Kit pressed the gas pedal to the floor and shot the car through the intersection. They barely missed a collision with a red convertible, but the SUV behind them, sufficiently intimidated by the near miss they'd had with the convertible, stayed right where it was. The van was trapped.

"I've always wanted to do that, too," Kit said. "Eddie Murphy ditched the cops who were tailing him with that trick."

Even as he spoke, he slammed on the brakes. The traffic ahead had come to a dead stop behind a delivery truck. Horns honked, drivers yelled curses, but no one moved.

"Damn," he said. "It worked better in the movies."

Precious seconds ticked away before Kit nosed the car into the other lane. Drew saw the light behind them change.

"The van just came through," she said.

"Time for an alternate strategy."

"Alternate strategy? That's just a fancy name for Plan C, right?"

"Very funny." She saw the dimples flash. "I like a woman with a sense of humor."

Gunning the engine, Kit leaned on the horn, then made a left turn right in front of an oncoming car. Drew was almost getting used to the blasting horns and screeching brakes they left in their wake. And she noted that Kit was still grinning like a madman as he threaded his way skillfully in and out of the traffic clogging the narrow street.

"You're enjoying this, aren't you?" she asked.

"Oh, yeah."

Maybe he wasn't crazy. Perhaps what she was looking at was a man giving free rein to his inner child. They were getting closer to the wharfs. She could see the Golden Gate Bridge illuminated in the distance, and traffic was slowing them down. The good news was that there was less chance of dying in a ten-car pileup. The bad news was that she thought she could see the van about a block behind them.

Without warning, Kit shot the car into a space at the curb and shoved the gear into Park. Turning to her, he grabbed her by the shoulders and gave her a hard kiss.

Crazy. He was definitely crazy, she thought. He drove like a lunatic and kissed like a god. Her heart was racing so fast that one beat blurred into the next. Soon the ache would begin to build. She wanted that. She wanted Kit.

The men chasing them weren't far behind. But all rational thought was being pushed aside by what her body wanted. Needed.

Instead of shoving him away, she grabbed fistfuls of his T-shirt and held on. It was Kit who finally drew back. She had to concentrate on unclenching her hands and letting him go.

"A sense of humor and nerves of steel. I'm beginning to think you're the girl of my dreams. Tell me you like baseball."

She stared at him as she tried to marshal her thoughts together. "Baseball?"

"If you're a Giants fan, I'll ask you to marry me."

She stared at him. "I don't know if I like baseball."

"Well, we'll just have to find out. It's a real sticking point with me. I couldn't marry a woman who didn't like the Giants."

And with that, he kissed her again, quick and hard, and got out of the car.

9

DREW'S HEAD WAS SPINNING and her knees were still weak when he opened the passenger door and helped her out. Ari bounded to the pavement behind her. She had enough wits about her to note that Kit was handing the car keys to a young man she guessed to be no more than seventeen or eighteen with dark hair pulled back into a short ponytail.

"Park the car in the usual place, Cato," Kit was saying.

Park the car? Drew reached into the backseat to retrieve the wedding dress and the tote. She didn't intend to let either out of her sight.

"If a van pulls up," Kit continued, "tell them that valet parking is full. Take a good look at them, and if they show up at the door, send Georgy in to let me know."

"Sure thing, Mister Kit." The young man turned to a boy of about ten or eleven. "You got that, Georgy?"

The kid flashed him a grin. "Sure thing."

Drew spotted the van inching its way down the street toward them, and the panic that had been pushed aside by the kiss firmly reasserted itself.

Then Kit's hand was on the small of her back again, urging her forward through a revolving door. *The Poseidon* was scrolled in black letters on the glass about a foot from her nose. They stepped into a large airy entrance space that served as a bridge between a busy bar and restaurant on the lower level and what appeared to be an upscale dining room on the upper level. Both areas had redbrick walls, but that was where the resemblance between them ended.

She had a better view of the dining room, where candles flickered on tabletops of honey-colored wood and paintings of seascapes adorned the walls. On the lower level, fishnets swung from the brick and she could hear the sounds of laughter and music. The wall beyond the hostess' desk was glass and offered a view of the Golden Gate Bridge.

When she could find her tongue, she said, "This is a restaurant."

"My family's." She didn't miss the pride in Kit's voice as he guided her toward the hostess' desk.

She felt as if she'd missed a step somewhere, so she dug in her heels. "Why are we here? We don't have time. That van—"

"Relax. We didn't come to eat. I told you I had an alternate strategy. Plan C. Instead of trying to outrun them, I'm going to try a little sleight of hand."

"You'd better watch him. He's good at that." The young woman standing behind the hostess' desk had a pixie face surrounded by short dark curls and the same incredible blue eyes as Kit. "You're supposed to be at the cabin fishing with Nik and Theo."

"Change of plans. Drew, this is my sister, Philly. Drew's a client."

"Uh-huh." Philly didn't sound convinced, and the look she gave Drew was both friendly and assessing.

"You're going to drool over her shoes," Kit warned.

Lifting her chin, Philly sent him a quelling look. "I

don't drool." But she wiggled around the desk to get a better look. "Wow! I'm definitely envious."

"Business looks good," Kit said.

Philly rolled her eyes. "We have it on good authority that a restaurant critic will be visiting Helena's restaurant tonight. Things are a bit tense in the kitchen."

"Helena's gotten nothing but rave reviews."

"She wants everything to be perfect." Philly stretched out a hand to take the dress bag from Drew. "Let me hang that up for you."

Drew tightened her grip on the bag. "Thanks, but I want to keep it with me."

Ari seized that moment to insert himself between Philly and Drew, and Philly dropped down to one knee to allow the dog to lick her face. "No need to be jealous, boy. I still—" She broke off suddenly and glanced up at Kit. "You've had some excitement. Ari's worried—" She frowned. "Something about driving too fast?"

Eyes wide, Drew shifted her gaze to Kit, but he kept his attention on his sister. "I told you Drew was a client. Someone's after her, and I need your help."

"Why didn't you say so?" Still keeping a hand on Ari, Philly rose to her feet.

"Drew needs your clothes."

Philly's eyebrows shot up. "You want me to hostess in my underwear?"

Kit grinned. "I'm sure it would double Dad's business."

"And Helena would have a fit."

"Relax. I'm not asking you to strip. I figured Drew could borrow the clothes you came to work in. The two of you are about the same size."

Philly gave Drew an assessing glance. "We are. But I

don't have anything fancy enough to go with those shoes—just jeans, a T-shirt and sneakers. They're in the storeroom off the kitchen."

"Thanks, sweetie." Kit leaned down to kiss her cheek. "And I need to leave Ari with you."

"No problem. I don't think he wants to go with you right now. He has a very placid nature, and you've frightened him."

"I frightened myself," Kit said.

When Drew found herself being dragged toward the stairs leading down to the bar, she dug in her heels, then stepped out of them and walked back to hand them to Philly. "Turnabout's fair play. Why don't you try these out? We're probably the same shoe size, too."

"Thanks!"

Drew had the satisfaction of seeing Philly's whole face brighten before Kit once more pulled her away.

"I may drool after all," she called after them.

Kit closed his hand firmly around Drew's upper arm and pulled her down the stairs. "You're a sweet person, Drew. You've made her day."

"How did your sister know about the fast car ride?"

"It's complicated. The short version is that Philly can talk to animals. As I mentioned, my aunt Cass—you'll meet her when I get you to the house—believes that my brothers, Philly, and I have all inherited some psychic ability from our mother. She died shortly after Philly was born. And Philly seems to have gotten the lion's share."

"Then you really do have psychic abilities?"

"Just the tingling sensation at the back of my neck when something important is going to happen."

"Like when you saw the van?"

"Yeah." He shot her look as they reached the bottom of

the stairs. "Earlier, I had a kind of premonition that you were coming, too."

Drew didn't have to reply to that because for a short time they were too occupied with making their way through the crowd. While Kit ran interference, Drew was bombarded by a myriad of impressions. There were tables and booths, all of which were filled. Glass doors on one of the walls opened onto a brick, paved patio where more tables were filled with people.

The clientele appeared to be a mix of locals and tourists. She figured the tourists were the ones with the guidebooks and the cameras. And everyone seemed to be having a good time. A small band played at the edge of a dance floor where a group of people moved in a semicircle. Their laughter could be heard above the music, and she felt a pang of envy at the pure fun they were having.

Then she mentally shook herself. She wasn't feeling sorry for herself, was she? She sincerely hoped that she wasn't that kind of person. She was going to remember who she was and get her life back on track. She hoped.

Suddenly they were at the bar, and her gaze riveted itself on the tall, broad-shouldered man who stood behind it. His hair was white, his face was lined, but he had the same blue eyes as Kit and Philly. When he threw back his head and roared at something one of his customers had said, Drew realized that he also had Kit's laugh.

Kit had reminded her of the images artists had captured of Greek gods; this man reminded her of Zeus himself.

The moment he caught a glimpse of Kit, he stepped out from behind the bar and wrapped him in a hard embrace. Then his gaze met hers and he winked. Something inside of her eased at the warmth of that gesture.

"Dad, this is Drew, my latest client. Drew, this is my father, Spiro Angelis."

"Welcome." Spiro took her hand and raised it to his lips. "My son doesn't come here often enough. Thank you for bringing him."

Completely charmed, Drew said, "You have a lovely restaurant."

Spiro grinned, and she caught the wink of dimples.

Then Kit put a hand on her arm and met his father's eyes. Something passed between them. She wasn't sure what, but Spiro finally nodded. "So that's how it is."

"Yes," Kit said.

Then Spiro turned back to study Drew. "You're not Greek."

"No. At least, I don't think so. I don't remember—"

"She doesn't remember who she is right at the moment," Kit explained.

Spiro's eyes twinkled. "Ah, a mystery woman."

Georgy suddenly pushed himself between Spiro and Kit. He was breathing fast. "A man—" he paused to suck in air "—he got out…of the van…at the corner. Cato is stalling him, asking him if he has a reservation."

Kit pulled a bill out of his pocket and handed it to the boy. "Good work."

Then he spoke to his father. "Cato parked my car in the usual place. I need your ride. I'm taking Drew to the house."

Drew saw curiosity bloom in Spiro's eyes, but all he said was, "You know where the keys are."

"Thanks."

"Introduce Drew to Helena. And be warned, she may be on the warpath. There's another critic going to give rave reviews to her food tonight."

"So we heard." Then Kit was pulling her away again through a door behind the bar and down a flight of stairs.

"Your father is charming," she said.

"My father was flirting with you."

"No, I mean…well, maybe a little."

"Don't pay him any heed. He's having a minor midlife crisis. Philly graduated from college in January, and Dad decided the time had come for him to sew some wild oats. He took a month off, went back to Greece and came home with Helena."

"Helena?"

"Yeah. My sister Philly believes that Helena came here because of Dad. She sees the whole thing in terms of Paris carrying off Helen—and it's turning out to be just as disastrous."

"Helena's beautiful, then?"

"And talented and she has a very independent spirit. She may be Greek, but she's not the traditional kind of Greek woman that my mother was. Dad convinced Helena to leave her job as executive chef at a hotel in Athens to come here and he'd help her open her own place. I don't think that she knew until she got here that her restaurant would be an extension of The Poseidon. It's led to a little friction between them. My aunt Cass agrees with Philly and thinks that they fell in love at first sight and that, because Dad hasn't dated since Mom died eighteen years ago, his skills with regard to handling women are just a bit rusty."

"So Helena followed her heart."

"That's the theory of the women in the family. And Dad was following his heart when he convinced her to come here. Philly claims that Dad had no intention of opening an upscale dining room until he met Helena. But they are two stubborn Greek people, and wherever their hearts are now, they're not in San Francisco. She thinks that they've both developed a bad case of cold feet. The end result is that they're engaged in a turf war over whose ideas are best for the restaurant. It doesn't help Dad's pride that Helena's ideas are usually brilliant."

The staircase emptied into a large, pristine and very efficient-looking kitchen. There were chefs in white suits and waitpeople in black trousers and white shirts moving quickly. Drew had the impression she was watching a well-oiled machine. Kit drew her along the edge of the room until they reached the spot where a woman with dark hair pulled into a bun was adding a delicately carved chocolate flower to a slice of cake.

"Perfect. There you go," she said to a waiter.

Drew couldn't take her eyes off the older woman. In profile, Helena was beautiful, tall and regal-looking with classic features. Drew guessed her to be in her late forties, and Kit's reference to Helen of Troy wasn't that far off the mark. It was little wonder that Spiro had come up with an excuse to tempt her to come with him back to San Francisco.

Helena stripped off her gloves and hugged Kit. "I thought you were going fishing." She turned her smile on Drew. "Are you the reason he's standing his brothers up?"

"I'm a client," she said. "I hope everything goes well for you tonight. You don't look a bit nervous."

Helena shrugged as she clasped Drew's extended hand. "I've done everything I can do. Now it's up to the Fates. Why don't you stay and see what you think? I'll ask Philly to find you a table."

"We can't," Kit said. "Drew's in a bit of a jam. She's

going to change into Philly's clothes and then we're borrowing Dad's ride."

Helena's eyebrows lifted. "He's letting you borrow his precious motorcycle? You should feel honored. I asked him if I could borrow it, and he told me it wasn't safe for a woman. What do you think of that?"

"I—"

Sensing that Kit didn't want to get in the middle of any disagreement between Helena and his father, Drew said, "Isn't that just like a man? If someone said that to me, I'd go out and buy my own."

"Really?" There was a beat of silence. Then beaming a smile at Drew, Helena took her hands and squeezed them. "I like you. If you're in a jam, Kit's a good man to rely on. He's competent and he has a knack for solving problems."

"Ms. Helena," one of the waiters said.

"Excuse me." Helena gave Drew's hands a final squeeze, then turned and strode away.

"You're a brave woman," Kit murmured. "One of the things that my brothers and I have learned is that it's best not to take sides in any of their battles. Do you think she'll really buy a motorcycle?"

"I hope so."

He grinned at her. "Would you?"

She thought about it. "Maybe. If I'd followed a man to another country and he was getting cold feet."

His grin widened. "Guts. I admire that in a woman. And you're going to need them."

Her eyes narrowed. "Why?"

"Because you're about to go for a motorcycle ride with a man who's never driven one."

10

"You're sure you've never driven one of these before?" Drew studied Spiro's motorcycle with a dubious expression on her face.

"Very sure." After removing the helmets, Kit managed to fit the wedding dress along with his gun and the tote in the carrying case at the back of the bike. "This is my virgin trip. Dad's only had this thing for a month, and I've been waiting for a chance to ride it." He handed a helmet to Drew.

"Maybe we should reconsider this." She glanced down the length of the alley. "There has to be another option."

"Cautious. I like that in a woman, too. C'mon." He took her hand and drew her down the short alley. A Dumpster blocked their view of the street. Carefully peering around it, he scanned the valet-parking lot that The Poseidon used and found what he was looking for. Then he squatted down and glanced back to Drew. "Stay behind me and take a look. See the van?"

He counted three beats before she said, "Yes. It's just around the corner."

"Good eyes. The driver's watching the lot while his buddy is looking for us inside." Kit paused as they watched a large, burley looking man approach the van and climb in on the passenger side. "Speak of the devil. I guess he's decided that we got away."

He barely got the words out before the van shot from the curb and turned the corner in a direction away from the restaurant.

"Are they giving up?" Drew asked.

"Looks like they are for now," Kit said. "Which may mean that they have another way of locating you."

"How?"

He turned to her. "If you left your purse behind at the church, one of them may have picked it up and they know where you live. If they figure we've given them the slip here, they can just go there and wait. In the meantime, we've got us a little reprieve."

"So we can use your car?"

He shook his head. "I'd rather play it safe."

She narrowed her eyes. "What you'd rather do is ride that motorcycle."

He grinned at her. "Well, there's that, too. And, now that we're not being chased, it might be fun. What do you say?"

She hesitated a beat. "Okay."

He gave her a quick kiss on the forehead. "The more time I spend with you, the more certain I am that you're my dream girl." And Kit was slowly realizing that he spoke nothing less than the truth. There wasn't much about Drew that he didn't like. Grabbing her hand, he urged her back to the bike.

She was lifting the helmet when he said, "Of course, it might help my driving skills if you kissed me for good luck."

She met his eyes then, and he waited. He wanted to kiss her again, but he was giving her a choice. He hadn't given her any the two times that he'd grabbed her and kissed her in the car. Caveman tactics weren't his usual style with women. Normally, he was a very patient man. Not that he'd been patient with her in his office; neither of them had been that. He liked to think of himself as a skilled but gentle lover. But his reaction, his response, to this woman had been different from the start. She was different.

Drew was studying him now with an intense look in her eyes as if she was determined to figure him out. "That's all I am right now…a 'dream girl.' We don't know who I am and what I may have done. And what happened between us—"

"Was amazing." He took her hand and brushed his lips over her knuckles.

"Yes. But it shouldn't have happened."

"Who ever knows for sure what the Fates have in store?"

I'm serious. I'm very possibly involved in a murder."

"No. I'm almost certain the person you shot managed to get away."

She gripped his hand hard. "I didn't kill anyone?"

"No." When relief flashed into her eyes, he cursed himself for not telling her sooner. Of course, they'd been a bit distracted since he'd come out of the church. "I'll give you a full report once I get you safely to my place. There were several shots fired at the church. The priest was one of the victims. He was shot by the altar. Another man was shot in the sacristy."

Horror filled her. "Did I shoot all of them?"

"No. There's a witness, the caterer, who saw the man who shot the priest. And I'd give you one-hundred-to-one odds that you weren't in the sacristy or at the altar. I'm pretty sure I found the room you remembered. It's in the choir loft where the bride waits with her attendants. There was blood there." He carefully omitted the fact that he believed two people had been shot in the room. There was no sense in telling her that until they knew more. "But no body. The only other casualty was my friend, Roman. But he wasn't shot. He took a fall over a staircase railing. Once he regains consciousness, he may be able to describe what happened. And you were right about the roses. The bridal bouquet was full of them."

"Was I the bride?"

It was his turn to grip her hand hard. "No. Her name is Juliana."

"And she's all right? What about the groom? Did they tell you who I am?"

"That's part of the mystery," Kit said. "They weren't at the church. They've vanished."

"Did the man I shot kidnap them?"

Kit studied her for a moment. "You've got a quick mind, sugar. That's certainly one possibility."

"And you mentioned the caterer? Did she know who I am?"

Kit shook his head. "She was unloading her van when she saw you get out of a taxi with the bride and go into the church. After that she was setting up stuff in the rectory dining room for a little reception. The priest had hired her, and she claims she'd never met the bride and groom— didn't even know their names. She had been prepared to serve them, the priest and two witnesses. I figure one of them was probably you. Why don't you save the rest of your questions until we get to my place?"

When she hesitated, he tucked a strand of hair behind her ear. "I could really use that good-luck kiss.'"

"You know what happened the last time we kissed."

His lips curved. "Yeah. But we'll have to stop with a kiss this time. We're in an alley."

She was still regarding him with that intent look of hers. There was a time when a fisherman had to be patient and wait for the fish to take the bait. But sometimes it helped to jiggle the line a bit.

"Just one kiss for the road?"

"Okay. But don't say I didn't warn you." With that, she set the helmet on the bike, placed her hands on his chest and rose on her toes. "You're going to have to meet me halfway on this."

He did, settling his hands on her waist to steady her and lowering his head until her lips could meet his. Kit let her control the kiss—the pressure, the angle, the depth—and focused all his attention on simply absorbing her. He thought he knew what to expect, but this time the sweetness was laced with raw greed, and it fueled his own response. He thought he was prepared, but when she threaded her fingers into his hair and pressed her whole body against his, the surge of heat nearly brought him to his knees. Too much, he thought. And not nearly enough. He staggered back against the wall, taking her with him.

She nipped his bottom lip and another explosion of heat erupted. He twisted so that her back was against the building. Desire seared through him. Sensations battered him. The soft sounds she made in her throat, the press of her nails into his shoulders, the quick catch of her breath when he bit her earlobe. The combination had his blood pounding.

He was drowning in her taste. Even as he searched her mouth for more, her flavors ripened, darkened, became

more addictive. Her scent no longer reminded him of soap
and water. Now he thought of rare flowers that only grew
in damp, steamy jungles. He thought of taking her on some
exotic beach late at night while waves crashed against the
shore. He thought of stripping her out of those jeans and
taking her here and now.

Even as the idea streamed into his mind, he gripped her
hips, lifted her and pressed himself against her, center to
center, heat to heat. Now, now, now, his mind screamed,
and he prayed that he could hold on to his control.

No woman had ever affected him this way. All he had
to do was look at her to want. All he had to do was taste
her, touch her, to crave. It was that simple. That primitive.

Now. Now. Now. Drew wasn't sure whether the word
was a chant in her mind or if she was murmuring it
against his skin as she raced her mouth over his neck and
sank her teeth into his earlobe. He was all she wanted. His
taste pouring into her, his hands—those strong clever
hands—at her throat, her breasts, her waist.

She couldn't think, couldn't breathe, couldn't remember
why she needed to do either. Was it always going to be this
way when he touched her? Stunningly different, haunt-
ingly familiar?

Now. Unclamping her legs, she slid down his body. As
need ripped through her, she tore at the snap of his jeans.
Then he was pulling at hers.

"This shouldn't be happening," she said, wondering
how she had the breath to get out the words.

"Definitely not."

Together they fumbled with the denim until they'd
managed to release him and free one of her legs from
her jeans.

"This is crazy. We're crazy. I thought it was just you, but I want you so much. I can't wait."

"Working on it," he muttered as he ripped foil off a condom and sheathed himself. Gripping her, he lifted her hips, and she locked herself around him. When she absorbed that first hard thrust, beneath the piercing stab of pleasure she felt the strange sensation of coming home.

Then the heat and speed engulfed her as they both began to move—faster, harder. He filled her vision, her mind, her world.

Then suddenly he stopped. And he stopped her. "Look at me, Drew, and tell me you're mine."

Her eyes narrowed on his. "Tell *me* you're mine."

"I'm yours." He began to move again until they both shattered.

AFTERWARD, Kit couldn't think. He couldn't walk. His breath was heaving in and out in gasps he couldn't control. She'd nearly destroyed him, and he'd cooperated fully.

At least he was still standing, still had her pressed against the wall. But he was trembling. Trembling. And for a moment when he'd been in her, with her, reality had slipped away entirely. They could just as easily have ended up lying in the debris on the floor of the alley.

The alley.

They'd just made love in an alley. Hadn't she said they were crazy? Had he hurt her? That question cleared the remaining sensual fog out of his mind. Easing her down, Kit stepped back, but he kept his hands on her shoulders and studied her. Her breathing was just as ragged as his, but she didn't look as if she were in pain. "Are you all right?"

She opened her eyes. "I…think so. My legs—are they still there? I can't feel them."

He glanced down. "Yeah." His were there, too. Then he met her eyes again. What could he say to a woman he'd just ravished in an alley? "This is a first for me."

She drew in a deep breath. "Under the circumstances, I can't be as certain of that as you are, but I hope I don't make a habit of this. I'm pretty sure bricks are permanently tattooed on my backside."

He couldn't prevent the laugh and was delighted when she joined him. It was at that moment that it struck him. He was falling in love with her. As the realization sank in, he watched her get her bare leg back in her jeans and locate a sneaker.

"It's ridiculous," she said.

It was that, all right, Kit thought, still bemused, still stunned.

"We can't go on this way. We have to figure out what to do."

"I think we just did." Kit zipped up his jeans.

"I'm serious." She waved a hand. "This is just… irresponsible. It was one thing to jump each other in your office. But we're in an alley. And who or what I am is still a mystery."

It was the word *irresponsible* that hit him hard. She was right. He'd never taken a woman with less care, less finesse. And it had been more than irresponsible—it had been damned reckless on his part.

Cupping the side of her face with his hand, he traced his thumb over her cheekbone. "I'm not being very careful of you."

"It's the kissing that starts it. We'd better not kiss again until this is over. Agreed?"

Kit met her eyes. "What I'll agree to is that you can make the call. If we kiss again and make love again, it'll be your decision." He watched her draw in a deep breath and let it out. She was a complicated woman, his Drew. Part of her was cautious and practical, but there was a part of her that would take a risk when it was warranted. Fascinating. He wouldn't make the first move no matter what it cost him. It wasn't sitting well with him that he'd taken her in an alley with two thugs looking for them.

"Time to go." He picked up her helmet and buckled it beneath her chin before donning his own. A fast ride was just what he needed to settle the emotions roiling through him.

He glanced up to see that she was still hesitating. Kit managed a grin. "C'mon. Look on the bright side. After what we just did to each other, I'm thinking this little ride will be anticlimactic."

"You're sure you don't have some kind of premonition that we're going to end up as roadkill?"

At her dry tone, his grin became genuine. "Nope. All I can see in the future right now is getting you to my place, pouring us two glasses of a very nice wine and fixing us the best omelet you've ever had. How does that sound?"

She shook her helmeted head. "You may not be as psychic as you think. What I'm envisioning is a quick stop at the hospital so that you can check on your friend. He may have regained consciousness by now."

Kit was moved that she would suggest it. "It could be risky. Those goons in the van got a good look at you at the church, and we still don't know who's behind this. I don't want to put you—"

"You think someone in Roman's family might be behind this?"

"No. But I don't want to take chances."

"Look. I'm wearing Philly's clothes, and I spotted a baseball cap in the compartment you stuffed the tote into. I'll push my hair into that."

He studied her for a moment. "Okay, but once we get to the hospital, I want you to do what I tell you, okay?"

"Okay."

As soon as she was settled behind him, her hands on his waist, he started the bike, pointed it at the far end of the alley and then opened up the throttle.

11

ANY THOUGHT Drew had of sitting primly behind Kit and keeping her hands on his waist for balance disappeared the moment they hit the first bump. After that, she wrapped her arms around him, shut her eyes and held on for dear life. Helena had said he was a competent man, she reminded herself as he pumped up the speed. Big, strong. And she'd experienced his exceptional competency in one area.

No, she was not going to think about making love with him again. But it was a tough resolution to stick to when she could feel his warmth through the thin T-shirt, feel his muscles bunch and then relax as he increased the speed.

Another bump set her adrenaline pumping and she sent up a little prayer that Kit Angelis had a fast learning curve when it came to the bike. After all, he *was* Greek. Hopefully, that meant he was a natural athlete. The Olympics had begun in Athens, right?

She heard the blast of a horn, a squeal of brakes and opened one eye in time to see Kit slice between two taxis, shoot around a truck and execute a smooth turn onto the embarcadero. Okay. He could steer pretty good, she decided. But in spite of that and the little pep talk she was giving herself, the lump of fear in her throat only dissolved when three more blocks had gone by and they were both still upright on the bike. Was she always such a nervous Nellie? she wondered.

But then, she hadn't let nerves deter her from making love to him. So far she hadn't exhibited any will power with regard to him. And was it any wonder? He was a beautiful man on so many levels and he wanted her. In spite of the trouble she was in. In spite of the fact that he didn't know anything about her.

When they stopped at the first traffic light, she drew in oxygen and forced herself to loosen the death grip she had on Kit just a little.

He turned. "You're safe. I could drive this little honey forever now that I've gotten the feel of it."

She'd gotten the feel of it, too, she realized. Not only that, she was beginning to like sitting behind Kit on the bike with the steady thrum of the motor beneath them.

She was still pondering that when he zipped the bike into the parking lot at the hospital and turned into an empty slot. She was off the bike and looking through the little trunk for the baseball hat when he stilled her hand. "I don't think that anyone here poses a threat to you, but once we get inside, I don't want anyone to know that we're together. You hang loose, but stay in my sight. Can you do that?"

"Sure."

Kit moved fast then, striding through the sliding doors to the lobby. Drew hung back, entering after Kit was already at the information desk. The lobby was clean, well lit and sparsely populated. She guessed that visiting hours were long over. She let Kit and a nurse enter the elevator before she followed.

When the doors opened on the fifth floor, a glassed-in waiting room was directly in front of them. She moved to a nearby water fountain and watched as Kit approached a distinguished-looking man with gray hair and a meticulously trimmed mustache. Roman's father? A taller man, younger and dark haired, stood next to him. Both were wearing suits and ties as if they'd just stepped out of a business meeting. There were others in the waiting room— a stunningly beautiful woman sat on a sofa with a young man sitting beside her. In a corner, a policeman raised his head from a newspaper to watch Kit as the older man wrapped him in a bear hug.

Realizing that she was staring, Drew moved into the waiting room and sank into the closest seat. The policeman glanced at her and then away. Kit and the two other men were speaking in low voices now. She could only catch a word here and there, but the tone wasn't good. A TV hung from the ceiling in one corner and she spotted the newswoman Kit had spoken to earlier on the steps of St. Peter's church. The volume was low, but the banner headline at the bottom of the screen was clear: *Murder and Mayhem at a Wedding.*

KIT KNEW EVEN as he approached Roman's father that the news wasn't good. Mario Oliver looked as if he'd aged ten years since Kit had last seen him. He recognized the other man as Michael Dano, who'd worked closely with Roman for the past three years. Dano, if Kit recalled correctly, headed up the legal department at Oliver Enterprises. So Sadie must work with him now.

Beyond them, he saw Roman's beautiful new stepmother, Deanna Mancuso Oliver, sitting on a couch with her son, Eddie. Kit knew from Roman that Deanna was in her late thirties, but she looked even younger, not nearly old enough to be the mother of a twenty-year-old son.

"Welcome, Kit." Mario hugged him, then gripped both of his hands.

"How is he?" Kit asked. "Can I see him?"

"Come." Mario led the way out of the waiting room and down the corridor. There was an officer at the door, but he made no move to stop them as they entered the room.

Roman was lying on the bed, his eyes closed. So still—that was the thought that moved through Kit's mind. Roman had always been so athletic, so active. If Kit hadn't known it was Roman, he might not have recognized his friend.

His face was pale, his head bandaged and he was hooked up to a series of monitors and tubes. Nik had said it was bad, but somehow Kit hadn't allowed himself to fully take that in—until now.

Please, let him be all right. The words repeated themselves in his mind as he moved closer to the bed and reached out to cover Roman's hand with his own. *Please.*

Kit was vaguely aware that Mario had followed him. When he felt the older man's hand on his shoulder, he whispered the question that was foremost in his mind. "Will he be all right?"

"The doctors are hopeful." Mario also spoke in a soft voice as he drew Kit away from the bed. "He has a skull fracture, so they're monitoring him closely. They're more concerned about the swelling at the base of the spine. If it doesn't go down by tomorrow, they're going to have to operate. In the meantime, they're keeping him sedated. They don't want him to move."

"Did he regain consciousness? Does he know what happened?"

"No," Mario said, "he hasn't come around yet."

After glancing at Roman again, Kit asked Mario, "Have you heard from Juliana or Sadie?"

"No." Mario's eyes narrowed. "Why do you ask? I haven't been able to reach them. Neither one is answering their cell phones. The police won't tell me a thing, but they're all over the place. I've got a couple of people trying to get me some information and I've got a call into the commissioner. Do you know what the hell is going on?"

For the first time, Kit noticed that Michael Dano had entered the room. Mario must have sensed something because he said, "It's all right. You can speak in front of Michael."

"No one told you about the wedding?"

Mario's eyes narrowed. "Wedding?"

As concisely as he could, Kit told them everything he knew about Juliana and Paulo's secret wedding plans and about the shootings at the church. The only thing he left out was the fact that he was working for the mystery woman.

Michael Dano interrupted at one point to mention that Channel Five news was covering a story about a wedding. The news team had been stationed in front of St. Peter's church giving live updates for the past hour, but that they hadn't given out any names yet.

Mario said nothing until Kit had finished. Before he spoke, he seemed to grow harder, as if he were gathering his strength. Kit had seen Roman do the same thing when the chips were down. And he could see in Mario's eyes the same keen intelligence.

Finally, Mario spoke. "My daughter Juliana and Paulo Carlucci were getting married and now they've disappeared?"

Kit nodded.

"And you think the police might blame Roman for what happened at the church?"

"Nik's afraid it's going to play out that way," Kit said. "I've put in a call to Theo. He's up at the fishing cabin and he isn't answering. I know that you have your own legal counsel, but—"

"Give me Theo's cell-phone number, will you?" Once he had, Mario asked, "And Sadie was at the church also?"

"It looks that way. She called me earlier and left a message on my machine. I haven't been able to reach her because she left her purse with her cell at the church."

"The Carluccis must be behind it," Michael Dano said.

Mario raised a hand. "What do you think, Kit?"

"Roman might have come there to stop the wedding, but if he shot someone it was in self-defense. I suspect that Roman might not have been the only one at the church with the idea of stopping the wedding, but I can't say who or why. It's just a theory."

Mario nodded. "The Carluccis have a lot of motivation to hurt me. I'm about to beat Angelo out of that land deal along the Orange County coastline."

"Once the Carluccis learn that Roman was there at the church, they're going to be thinking you're behind it," Kit pointed out. "What happens if the feud between the two of you gets hotter and more blood flows? Would that affect the land deal?"

Mario pulled a cigar out of his pocket and clamped his teeth around it, but didn't light it. After a moment, he turned to Michael Dano. "I want you to get back to the office and make sure that everything is all set for that deal to close."

Michael frowned. "The papers are all but signed. The money changes hands on Monday."

Mario's tone grew softer. "Just do what I say."

When Michael had left, Mario put a hand on Kit's shoulder. "Michael's a good man, but you think like my Roman."

"He'll be all right. He's tough."

Mario's eyes narrowed. "But…"

Kit rubbed the back of his neck. "I just have a feeling that there's another shoe that's going to drop."

Mario nodded. "One of your 'feelings.' Roman told me about them. You're working on this?"

Kit nodded. "So is Nik. And I'll get in touch with Theo. You'll keep me informed?"

"And vice versa," Mario said.

"Watch your back," Kit warned.

Together they walked back to the waiting room. Drew was at the water fountain. Mario was picking up one of the phones in the waiting room before Kit turned and punched the elevator button.

"YOU READY FOR another ride?" Kit asked when Drew caught up to him at the bike.

He hadn't said a word on the ride down in the elevator. And she could still recall the look on his face when he'd come out of Roman Oliver's room. She glanced at the bike and then at Kit. "I have a feeling that another ride on this motorcycle will be a lot easier for me than that visit was for you. How is your friend?"

He drew in a breath and let it out. "They don't know. I don't know."

Drew slipped her hand into his.

"He's such an active man. He can beat Theo at tennis. Nik and I can't do that. He's nearly as good a sailor as Nik. I'm better at fishing, but Roman has more of a talent for it than either Nik or Theo."

He was speaking of Roman as if he were a part of his family. She tightened her grip on his hand.

"It was hard to see him that…still."

"What did his father say?" she asked.

When he'd finished telling her, she was relieved to see that some of the tension had eased from his shoulders. "You'll know more in the morning."

Kit nodded. "I'm glad I came. At least his father knows what's going on. The police hadn't even let him know about the wedding or that his daughters are missing."

She heard the anger in his voice. "Do you want to stay here for a while?"

He shook his head. "There's nothing more that I can do here." Then he raised her hand to his lips. It was the briefest of contacts and it shouldn't have sent a ripple of heat through her. But it did.

Kit handed her a helmet and was about to put his own on when his cell phone rang. After glancing at the caller ID, he said, "It's Theo."

As she watched him fill his brother in on Roman's condition and what had happened at the church, Drew noticed his tension ease. He seemed to be close with his brothers, and she couldn't help but wonder if she had brothers or sisters of her own.

"Mario might bring Theo in on this." Kit said as he pocketed his cell. "I'd feel a lot better if he did."

Without another word, Kit put on his helmet, climbed on the bike and waited for her to mount behind him. As soon as she had, he backed the bike out of the parking place, eased it out of the lot and then opened the throttle. "Hold on."

This time it wasn't fear she felt, but a little pump of excitement. Traffic was moving more steadily and quickly now, and Drew shoved other thoughts and concerns out of her mind, quite willing to give herself up to the moment. The wind on her skin was cool, the speed exhilarating. The lights of the city flew past. Over her shoulder, she caught a glimpse of the illuminated Golden Gate Bridge. Farther on, a digital clock on a building told her that the time was 10:52 p.m. and the temperature was still eighty-seven degrees.

Kit slowed for another light. To her left, the pier was still alive with activity. Pier 39, she realized, and she wondered how she could be so sure of that and still not know who she was. Snatches of music drifted to the street. The stores on the pier were built on different levels and housed restaurants as well as shops. On the top level, she could see diners sitting at outside tables. Had she ever eaten there? On the lower level, people strolled along as if they hadn't a care in the world; others leaned against the railing or shot photos.

For a moment, she felt a sharp wave of envy as her own situation came back to her. Then she firmly shoved all of that out of her mind. For the length of the ride, at least, she was going to live in the moment.

As Kit stopped the bike, she caught a flash of white on the upper level. She had time to register that it was a young woman in a sundress before her vision blurred and her head spun.

The images shot into her mind—just as fast and just as detailed as the last time. There were shadows again but they weren't nearly as dark. The musty smell was gone. In its place was a heavy floral scent—not of fresh flowers, but of a perfume. She heard the soft strains of music and, through glass doors in front of her, she saw rain streaming down. Two figures pushed through the doors, a young man and a woman, holding hands and laughing as water dripped off of them. They were so young. And so radiantly happy that her breath caught in her throat. She knew them… She was sure of it. But before she could remember their names, the image vanished.

KIT STOOD beside Drew, gripping her arms as she opened her eyes. She seemed surprised that he'd pulled the bike up on the sidewalk against a railing that looked out on the sea.

"You okay?" he asked.

"I remembered something more."

"Yeah. I figured. Lucky thing we were stopped at a light. You nearly fell off, and then I would never have heard the end of it." While he talked, he engaged the kickstand and helped her off the bike and down beside him on the curb. "Tell me what you remembered."

"Here?"

"Right here. We're not getting back onto that motorcycle until you've got some more color in your cheeks." That much was true. But it was also true that he didn't want to let go of her yet. Not until his heartbeat steadied. When he'd felt her sag against him, he hadn't been sure that he could keep her from toppling into the street.

"I wasn't at the church this time. At least, I don't think I was."

"Close your eyes and tell me the details."

When she'd finished describing the scene, he said, "It

was raining, you heard music, smelled women's perfume, and this young, beautiful couple came in through a glass door. Did I leave anything out?"

"I had a feeling that I knew them." She pressed a hand against her temple. "But I can't come up with their names. It's so close. Why can't I remember."

Kit squeezed her shoulders. "You will. Could be they're the bride and groom. You have to have known at least the bride since you arrived with her at the church last night. My best guess is that you were the maid of honor. Does the name Carlucci mean anything to you? Paulo Carlucci?"

"No. It doesn't mean anything."

"How about Juliana Oliver?"

She shook her head again. "She's related to your friend?"

"Yes. His baby sister."

"And she's missing? Oh, Kit, I'm so sorry."

"I know." And the fact that she cared was a comfort to him. But he wanted her to concentrate on the memory while it was still fresh. "Tell me what kind of music was playing? Rock? Reggae? Rap?"

He watched as a little line appeared on her forehead, a sign that she was thinking hard. Odd that he'd known her for such a short amount of time and yet he knew that about her.

"Classical. Piano. Maybe Chopin. And it was soft. Very…discreet."

"Probably piped in. And the doors were glass—the kind you push through. Maybe you were in the lobby of a hotel or a restaurant. Chopin's a little upscale for a bar or a club."

She met his eyes. "You're very good at this."

He grinned at her. "Didn't I tell you that I was the best?"

She smiled at him, and Kit felt his heart do a strange

little somersault. "C'mon," he said as he rose and helped her to her feet. "I'm going to quit while I'm ahead. Besides, I'll feel safer when I get you to my place."

_12_

"THIS IS WHERE you live?" Drew stared at the three-story house with its tower thrusting up into the sky. It was set back from the road at the end of a wide, circular drive and surrounded by shade trees, neatly trimmed hedges and what looked like at least an acre of lawn. To the left of the house, the yard sloped gently down to a large pond.

"Yeah. But not just me." Kit took her hand and drew her up the front steps. "The whole Angelis family lives here. It's my aunt Cass's house. She's my mother's sister and their grandfather, my great-grandfather, immigrated to this country from Greece in the 1920's and started a shipyard that did well enough for him to build this place."

"It's lovely." In the moonlight it reminded her of a place where a princess might live.

The front door was outlined in etched glass and opened into a wide hall that boasted a carved-oak staircase. The wood gleamed in the light from a crystal chandelier.

"It takes a lot of money to keep the place up, more money than Aunt Cass makes with her psychic consultations, and Dad puts a lot of the restaurant money back into the business, so my brothers and I pay rent now. So does Aunt Cass's son, Dino, when he's home. He's in the Navy so he travels a lot. Five years ago, we pitched in and renovated the place into apartments. Aunt Cass and Philly have apartments on the main floor. My brothers and I live on the second and third floors and Dad has the gardener's cottage. We figure when we move out—which I assume we all will eventually—Aunt Cass can rent the apartments out. Theo did the math, and the income should provide her with enough money for a very comfortable retirement."

He pressed a hand to her back as they started up the stairs. "My place is on the second floor."

His place turned out to be a large airy room, lined on three walls with bookshelves. Two leather couches faced each other in front of a fireplace and the fourth wall was split by three tall windows. Kit led her to one of the couches.

"Sit," he said as he draped his jacket over the back of the couch and set his gun carefully down on one of the shelves. "I'm going to open a bottle of wine and then I'll fix you that omelet I promised you."

Sinking into the soft cushions of the couch, Drew watched as Kit moved to a cabinet in the bookcase, extracted a wine bottle and uncorked it. He filled two glasses and handed one to her as he sat down beside her.

"You've been very patient with me. So I think before I make that omelet, I should fill you in on what I've been able to discover about what went on at that church."

She took a quick sip of her wine and felt much better when he took her hand. "The bride is Juliana Oliver, and the groom is Paulo, the son of Angelo Carlucci." Kit gave her a brief history of the rivalry between the Carlucci and Oliver families.

"You think Juliana and Paulo are the couple I remember coming in through those glass doors?"

"Could be. You said they were young. Paulo's about

twenty and Juliana is even younger, and their families would do anything they could to prevent the marriage."

"Shades of Romeo and Juliet," she said.

"Good analogy. The feud between the Montagues and the Capulets probably had nothing on the one between the Olivers and the Carluccis. If the news got out about the wedding—and it evidently did—both families would have a motive for putting a permanent end to the marriage."

She tightened her hand on the wineglass. "Permanent as in…"

"Killing the bride or the groom or both? Maybe."

Drew thought for a minute. "And the police suspect Roman of coming to the church with that in mind?"

"At the very least, they're going to think that he came to the church to stop the wedding. The fact that he brought a gun and fired it doesn't look good for him. When I spoke with Nik, his theory was that Roman and Paulo struggled at the top of the stairs and Roman fell over the railing to the vestibule floor."

"Do you think that Roman went there to stop the wedding?"

Kit ran a hand through his hair. "Perhaps. He's going to take over the business for his father one day. I don't imagine that he would be happy about his sister's choice of a bridegroom. But he wouldn't have gone there to shoot anyone. What worries me is that the police are going to be under a lot of pressure to put this case to rest. And Roman can't defend himself. They're keeping him sedated until they decide whether or not to operate to relieve the swelling on his spine. By the time he can tell his side of the story, the police will have built a pretty good case against him." He paused to rub the back of his neck. "And

I have a feeling that there's more bad news coming down the pike."

She put a hand over his. "Do you want to go back to the hospital? I could stay here."

Something moved through Kit when he saw the concern in her eyes. He wanted to pull her into his arms and just hold her, but he clamped down on the impulse. "Thanks, but I'm not leaving you. The best thing I can do for Roman right now is to stick with you. Once you recover your memory, we're going to know a lot more about what went on in that church."

She was going to argue with him, he saw it in her eyes, but a knock on the door forestalled her.

Rising, Kit kept hold of her hand and drew her toward the archway that opened off the room. "Wait here in the kitchen." It was unlikely that they'd been followed, but there was a possibility that the two goons had traced his license plate, and he wasn't taking any chances.

He retrieved his gun. "Who is it?"

"It's your aunt Cass."

Relieved, Kit tucked the gun into the back waistband of his jeans and opened the door.

She handed him two plastic grocery bags. "Just a few things for the omelet you're going to make."

Kit studied her for a moment. She looked perfectly composed and serene the way she always did. She was a tall woman, not beautiful in the way that Helena was. Still, her features were classic and, in her late fifties, Cassandra Angelis was still stunning. However, it was her eyes that fascinated him. They were a deep amber color, and he'd always had the feeling that they could see right into him. Tonight, her gray hair was pulled back from her face and she had on one of the flowing caftans that she usually wore during her appointments. He didn't bother to ask how she'd known that he was thinking of making an omelet. He'd accepted his aunt's ability to know things long ago.

A sudden possibility occurred to him. "Drew, it's safe to come out. I'd like you to meet my aunt, Cassandra."

He studied his aunt's face as Drew walked toward them. "Aunt Cassandra, this is my client, Drew. I don't suppose you know her last name?"

"Please, call me Cass." She took Drew's extended hand in both of hers and paused for a minute. Then she smiled and nodded. "Yes. Yes, indeed. I don't know your last name… yet, but you'll find the answers you're seeking by the end of the weekend." She turned to Kit. "And so will you."

Kit glanced at Drew. "It was worth a shot. She's the real McCoy when it comes to having psychic powers and seeing the future."

Cass kept her eyes on Drew. "It's like seeing through a glass darkly. Similar to the way you're picturing your memories."

Drew's eyes widened. "You know about that?"

"I sensed it as soon as I took your hand." Releasing Drew, she shifted her gaze to Kit. "I have to go back to my office. One of my clients will be calling shortly. And since you'll want to talk to Nik, why don't you take him one of those bags? His cupboard is usually as bare as Mother Hubbard's."

The moment Cass left, Kit turned back to Drew. "Stay here. Lock the door and don't open it until I get back. Promise?"

"Sure."

He closed the door behind him and waited until he heard the lock click before he hurried up the stairs. He nearly ran into Nik at the top.

"What are you doing here?" They spoke in unison.

"Aren't you busy with the case?" Kit added.

Nik scowled at him. "Parker took me off it. He's going to head up the investigation himself. Turns out the caterer, J. C. Riley, is the mayor's daughter. Since she can identify the man who shot the priest, the commissioner and her father want her protected twenty-four-seven. Parker picked me for the job."

Kit's eyebrows shot up. "The woman you handcuffed to the radiator is the mayor's daughter?"

He glared. "I don't care if she's the president's daughter. She refused to stay put, and she wouldn't shut up and I had a crime scene to investigate. And how do you know I handcuffed her?"

Kit raised both hands, palms out. "I went out through the sacristy. You told me to take the back stairs, remember?"

Nik huffed out a breath. "Yeah, yeah."

Kit studied his brother. To his knowledge, Nik had never had a problem with a woman in his life. He could be tough when dealing with a female suspect, but he had always operated very smoothly with the opposite sex. Since Nik was three years his senior, Kit had learned a lot from observing his brother's techniques. The redheaded caterer had definitely rubbed him the wrong way.

"So you brought her here?" Kit asked. He could understand that. He'd done the same thing with Drew.

"The commissioner's right about one thing," Nik said. "She can ID one of the shooters, and he'll want to eliminate her."

Just then, the pretty caterer poked her head out of Nik's door. "Hey, Slick, I'm starving here." She beamed a smile at Kit. "Hi there, good cop."

"Hi." Kit handed the grocery bag to Nik. "Aunt Cass had a feeling you'd be in need of food."

"Of course she did." Nik carried the bag to the mayor's daughter. "I think you'll find everything you need. I'll be just a minute."

When the door closed, Kit said, "Slick?"

"Good cop?" Nik strode back to his brother, his eyes narrowing.

Kit raised his hands again as Nik backed him into a wall. "All I did was ask her a few questions. I swear."

When Nik drew back, Kit asked, "You got any new info about what went on at the church?"

"Anything specific you're interested in?"

"Has Father Mike been questioned?"

"I don't have any news on that yet," Nik said with a scowl.

"Have you ID'd the man who was shot in the sacristy?"

"Gino DeLucca, Paulo Carlucci's bodyguard. And the bullet that killed him probably came from Roman's gun. Ballistics hasn't confirmed it yet, but the make of the gun matches the bullet. Parker will use that as evidence that Roman came to stop the wedding."

"If Roman shot DeLucca, it was in self-defense," Kit said. "Or to protect Juliana. The only thing that makes sense is that someone besides Roman got wind of the wedding and tried to put a stop to it."

"I tend to agree, but Parker and the commissioner are favoring exactly what I told you at the church—Roman got wind of the wedding, became furious with his sister and came to stop it. They'll figure he brought some firepower with him and Paulo pushed him over the railing of those stairs."

"What happened to the bride and groom?"

"They haven't shown up yet."

"Any word about Sadie?"

"No."

"What about the mystery woman?"

"No word on her, either."

"Roman might have come to stop the wedding. But he wouldn't bring armed men with him and he wouldn't have given orders to shoot the priest. Someone else is behind this."

Nik put a hand on his brother's shoulder. "You know that and I know that."

"I went to see him at the hospital."

Nik's hand tightened.

"He doesn't look good," Kit continued. "And I hate the fact that he's lying there defenseless while a case is being built against him. Theo called and I filled him in."

Nik met his eyes steadily. "We're going to find out what really happened."

Kit studied him for a moment. "You're not going to stay out of it, are you?"

He flashed a grin. "Hell, no. Not any more than you are, bro. Roman's like a part of this family. Besides, anyone who can beat our Theo at tennis is all right." Then his expression sobered. "I want to find out who's behind this as much as you do. There's a lot we don't know yet. And I'm beginning to think that the mystery blonde who arrived with the bride holds the key." Nik paused, then added, "What? Did you find something out about the blonde?"

Nik's eyes were altogether too sharp, Kit decided. "No.

I'm as interested in her as you are. First thing in the morning, I think I'll try to track down her identity."

"Good idea. Keep me informed." He strode to his door, then glanced back. "And wish me luck."

"Me, too," Kit replied as he turned and descended the stairs.

AFTER LOCKING THE DOOR, Drew paced the room. Her mind was so filled with worries and fears that her head was spinning. Kit had discovered quite a bit at the church. There'd been at least one other shooter—the man who'd shot the priest. And Kit had said she was probably a friend of the bride. It made sense that if she'd shot someone, it was to protect Juliana or herself. If so, the person she'd put a bullet into was probably a bad guy. She'd feel a lot better about it if she'd shot a bad guy.

Drew glanced at the tote that she'd set down near the door. That nice little scenario didn't take into account the money. Or why she'd fled from the scene.

No. She was not going to let her imagination run wild again. The facts. Hadn't Kit told her to stick to the facts? In the jumble of information and possibilities, the one and only thing they were sure of was that someone was after her. And that argued that she'd gotten on the wrong side of some bad guys. The good news and bad news all rolled into one.

Crossing to the coffee table, she picked up her wine and took a sip. She'd have to remember to laugh at that some day. And there would be a "some day" when she'd know who she was, a day when she'd get her life back.

Maybe she could hurry it along. Sinking down on the arm of the couch, Drew closed her eyes and tried to summon up what she knew about that room in the church. Shadows, darkness, the musty scent…

The smell of old books had the panic bubbling in her stomach. She felt the cold metal of the gun against her palm, pictured the door opening slowly. Fear snaked through her, numbing her mind, freezing her blood. The ache in her head began to build. She willed it away, and tried to see who else was there…but it was too dark and she could feel her finger squeezing the trigger.

Pain knifed through her head, and she pressed her fingers to her temples to ease it. Gritting her teeth, she ordered more details to appear, but the memory didn't get any clearer and the pain grew steadily worse. Unable to stand it anymore, she opened her eyes and blinked to clear her vision.

Bookshelves. She was in Kit's apartment, and the wall in front of her was filled with books, framed pictures and odds and ends. The details of a person's life.

A photo caught her attention. It was a picture of Kit standing on a dock with a fishing pole in his hand. He was bent over so far that it nearly touched the water. His feet were planted wide on the dock and there was tension in every line and angle of his body. Whoever had snapped the photo had captured a battle at its peak. And from the look on Kit's face, she guessed that he'd won it. He was a man you could depend on to see things through.

In the framed photo next to it, she recognized Philly in a cap and gown with Spiro on one side of her and Cass on the other. Kit stood to the left of his father and two other men stood to the right of Cass. They had to be Kit's brothers. One of them was shorter than the other two and could best be described as rugged. The other brother was taller and his looks bordered on the pretty. She suspected his suit was Italian, and he had the polished look of a male model. Kit and the rugged-looking man were dressed more casually in khaki slacks and sport coats.

Any way you sliced it, the Angelis brothers were definitely lookers. And they belonged to a close-knit family. Was her family like that? Why couldn't she remember them?

Struggling against a wave of frustration, Drew set the photo back on the shelf. Whoever she was, she'd deal with it. Hadn't Kit said that she was a lady? She glanced down at her hands. She evidently took good care of herself. Had she been born into a fairly well-to-do family? Or was she a self-made woman?

She preferred the latter. She wanted very much to be independent, the kind of woman who made her own way, who didn't lean on others too much for support.

Rising, she began to pace again. The truth was, her past was a blank. Her future was a blank. The only thing she had to judge herself against was right now.

And right now, her life was a mess. She was a mess. She knew enough to know that what was blocking her memory was fear. Each time she got close to something, it blindsided her. Did that mean she was a coward? Kit had said that she was cautious, but that she also had shown courage. True, she'd gone to his office. But what other choice did she have? And ditto for her "courage" in climbing on the motorcycle. All that proved was that when her back was to the wall, she'd take a risk. How about otherwise?

She thought not. Case in point—her attraction to Kit Angelis. He was leaving the choice to her and she'd told him they'd better not kiss again.

But she wanted him to kiss her again. She wanted him

to make love to her. And she wanted to make love to him right back. Just thinking about running her hands over those hard muscles, that smooth skin, had her insides melting and an ache staring to build deep in the core of her.

When he walked in that door, she'd have a choice to make. Would she risk it or would she run? Just thinking about it had the nerves tangling in her stomach. It wouldn't be long before she learned something about herself in the present.

13

KIT HESITATED outside the door of his apartment. He knew exactly what he wanted to do when he went back in there—and it wasn't cook omelets. What he was hungry for had nothing to do with eggs and cheese.

But he'd promised that he'd let her make the choice. He always let the woman make the final choice, but he was pretty good at guiding them toward it. He liked to think that he had some skills in the art of seduction. But in this instance, he wasn't sure it would be fair to…

What? Charm her? Seduce her? Reel her in like a fish? Disgusted with himself, he turned and paced the short distance to the staircase.

She wasn't just another woman. She was Drew—a woman smack-dab in the middle of a serious mess. The men in that van had wanted to get their hands on her. And he'd taken her to The Poseidon and introduced her to his family, for heaven's sake. That one fact should have been enough to make him back off.

Still, if—no—*when* he walked back into his apartment, he wasn't altogether certain that he could keep his promise to her. The first time he'd turned and seen her in the doorway to his office, an ache had begun inside of him and he couldn't seem to shake it loose. He remembered what it felt like to hold her in his arms, to taste her, to lose himself in her. Just thinking about it sharpened the ache almost unbearably and filled his mind with images of what he wanted to do to her, with her.

And he couldn't do any of them because he'd told her that whatever happened next between them would be up to her.

What in hell had possessed him to do that? Because she was a damsel in distress and he kept thinking of himself as some white knight who was going to rescue her? Well, courtly chivalry had definite drawbacks. Hell, here he was standing in the hallway dithering like an old lady. Kit ran a hand through his hair. No woman had ever made him dither before.

A little flame of anger began to burn inside of him. Who said he had to be a white knight? All he had to do was march in there and renegotiate. He'd simply tell her that he'd thought he could let her make the choice but he wanted her to release him from the promise. That he wanted to make love to her. His decision made, he strode toward the door and lifted his hand to knock.

Dammit. What was he thinking? He couldn't do that. He was a man of his word. He couldn't just say, "Hey, I made a mistake. I've changed my mind."

For a moment he closed his eyes and resisted the urge to pound his head against the door. What he would do was go in there and feed her. Then he'd update her on what Nik knew so far. It was almost midnight, the witching hour, so after he fed her, he'd tell her that they should both get some sleep. Who knew—if she got some rest, she might wake up in the morning with her memory restored.

And he might wake up with an ability to think a little

more objectively. It was a plan. Kit raised his hand and knocked on the door.

It swung open so fast that he knew she'd been standing right on the other side. He frowned. "I thought I told you not to open the door unless you knew it was me."

"I looked through the peephole and saw it was you." The breathlessness in her voice made him really look at her. Her hands were clasped tightly in front of her in a way that told him her nerves were stretched tight. "What happened? Did you remember something else?"

"No. I tried, but it didn't work."

There was a tenseness in her shoulders and something in her eyes, in her stance, that made him think fleetingly of Athena ready for the hunt. The ache sharpened inside of him again.

"I just decided something."

Remember your battle plan, Angelis. "Why don't you tell me about it while I start those omelets?"

"Wait."

He tried to move around her. When she stepped sideways, he came up against her body. Not good for the plan.

She didn't step back and neither did he. The fact that her scent was now wrapping around him boded even worse for the plan.

"I'm not hungry. I mean…I'm not hungry for food."

Kit went absolutely still. So did the room. In fact, the silence was so complete that he thought he could hear the tick of his great-grandfather's clock on the mantel. He could also hear the sound of his blood trickling a few drops at a time out of his brain.

She drew in a deep breath, and he thought of Athena again, ready to do battle.

"Remember what I told you in the alley—that we shouldn't kiss again?"

"Yeah."

"Well…" When she paused to moisten her lips, he had to swallow a moan.

"I've changed my mind. I want you to kiss me again. I mean…if you still want to?"

The blood wasn't trickling now, Kit decided. It was gushing. "Yeah, I still want to." About as much as he wanted to go on breathing. But he had enough functioning brain cells to note that she was wound tight with nerves and looked like she was getting ready to face a firing squad. Instinct told him that whatever inner battle she'd waged before he'd come back wasn't over quite yet. "Why did you change your mind?"

Her eyes narrowed and her chin lifted. "Do you have to investigate everything?"

Relief sang through him at the flash of temper in her eyes. "It's been a habit since I was a kid."

"Okay." Drew whirled away and began to pace the short distance between the door and the couch. "I changed my mind because I want you. There's nothing else that I can be certain of in my life right now, except for that. And because if I don't grab this chance to make love with you again, I might not get another one. We could learn something horrible about me—you might not want me then."

She spun around and faced him, hands fisted on her hips, her foot tapping. "Plus, there's the fact that you're a gorgeous, sexy, desirable man. And you certainly acted in your office and in that alley as if you wanted me."

She strode back to him and poked a finger into his chest. "Last. but not least, I don't want to think that I'm the kind of woman who wouldn't grab an opportunity like this. I'm going to absolutely hate it if I turn out to be a wimp. There." She poked him again. Then she grabbed two fist-fuls of his T-shirt. "Does that satisfy your curiosity? Can we get on with this now?"

Kit thought she was magnificent.

"You got it, sugar."

HER HEART WAS RACING so fast, Drew was surprised that it didn't shoot right out of her body. All her remaining doubts and reservations had drained away at some point during the little rant he'd driven her into. She wanted this beauti-ful man. If there was a price to pay, she'd worry about it later.

Releasing her grip on his shirt, she reached up, pulled down his face and imprisoned his mouth with hers. His lips were firm and warm and, once she parted them, his taste sparked a storm inside of her. This is what she'd been craving—the heat, the threat, the promise.

His hands gripped her waist. Finally, she thought. Then without breaking contact, he moved, turning her as if they were dancing. Head spinning, she heard the door close and felt the press of the wall against her back. All the while, sensations swirled through her. His mouth was so hot, so delicious, she could have gone on exploring it for a long time. As if sensing her intent, he took control of the kiss. His lips were so hard, so sure, his teeth so gentle as he nipped her bottom lip and sent a shock wave of pleasure right down to her toes.

His thumb tipped up her chin as he changed the angle of the kiss and let his tongue do a seductive dance with hers. Drew nearly cried out in protest when he dragged his mouth away from hers, but the scrape of his teeth on her throat had her breathing his name instead. He pulled her to him so that she could feel his erection, know how ready he was. The knowledge increased the hunger inside of her.

Suddenly, he drew back, gripping her shoulders to steady her against the wall. They were both gasping for breath. The heat in his gaze nearly seared her flesh.

"Kiss me again," she demanded.

"I will, but I think we ought to slow this down a bit."

"Why? Fast has been working very well."

His lips curved slightly. "I agree. We'll revisit fast… eventually." Kit lifted her hand and turned it over. "There are advantages to going slowly." When he pressed his mouth to her palm, she felt each separate sensation, the whisper of his breath, the moist warmth of his mouth all the way through her.

"There are things I've been thinking about doing to you. Other things I want you to do to me."

"Oh." Her stomach suddenly sank as a thought struck her.

He drew a finger down her forehead. "What's worrying you now?"

"It's just that…" What if she was lousy in bed? "I might not be very good at this. I mean—I don't remember if I am."

"You've been doing great so far."

"There's not much technique involved in fast."

"Ouch."

She felt heat flood her cheeks. "I didn't mean… I'm not complaining. You're…amazing. It's me."

"I've got an idea. If it's technique you're worried about, I could teach you. We'll play follow the leader. I'll do something to you, and then you do the same thing to me. That should slow things down a bit, so that I don't just give in to my instincts and take you against the wall again. What do you think?"

She couldn't think, at all—not while images of him pinning her against the wall and pushing himself into her poured into her mind. If she hadn't been leaning against that wall, if he hadn't been holding her, she'd have slid to the floor in a little pool of lust. "Sure," she finally said, even though she wasn't *sure* what she was agreeing to.

"First, I'm going to get you out of some of these clothes. Watch closely."

She glanced down. His hands were curved around her waist, his thumbs meeting at her naval. He moved them upward, slowly. The T-shirt moved with them until his thumbs paused right in the valley between her breasts. Her breasts hardened in anticipation and her insides clenched. Finally, he slid his thumbs beneath the shirt and rubbed them over her nipples. She wanted him to do more than that, but instead, he pulled the shirt over her head and simply looked at her.

"I've spent quite a bit of time wondering just what you were wearing under that suit, and I had an idea that it would be fancy and lacy." He ran a finger lightly along the lace at the top of her bra. Just that featherlike touch made something contract deep inside of her.

He must have seen something in her expression because he said, "Lovemaking is better when all the senses are involved—sight and sound and taste as well as touch. Watching me touch you arouses you, doesn't it?"

"Yes." And that was a huge understatement. His hands were strong, masculine, his skin shades darker than hers.

The contrast as his thumbs moved over her nipples was erotic. Tearing her gaze away, she glanced up to see that he was watching the movement, too, and his eyes had darkened. The pulsing inside of her quickened.

With one finger he traced the border of lace again, and little ripples of fire and ice raced along her nerve endings.

"I was wondering if your bra would match your thong. I have a weakness for sexy underwear." Drawing his hands slowly down to her waist, he hooked fingers into the waistband of her jeans and pulled the snap loose. Her breath quickened as the rasp of the zipper being slowly lowered filled the room. The sight of his hands pulling her jeans apart combined with the sound was incredibly erotic. But so was the warmth of his fingers against her stomach.

"Nice." His voice sounded a bit hoarse.

So did hers when she said, "Touch me. Please."

"My pleasure." Flattening one hand on her stomach, he slid it between her legs. "You're so wet. So hot."

Heat shot through her. Pressing her hands flat against the wall, she arched into his hand.

"Look at me, Drew."

She did. His jaw had hardened and his eyes were so dark that she could barely see the blue.

"I want to be inside you. Soon." He slipped one finger beneath the lace and pushed it into her. "Like this."

She had to grip his waist hard so that she wouldn't fall. "Now," she managed to say. "Come in right now."

But he didn't. Instead, he removed his hand and took a careful step back. "Your turn."

It took her a minute to recall the little game she'd agreed to play. Follow the leader. It was her turn to touch him the way he'd touched her. Thinking about it made her throat go dry as dust.

He was just standing there, waiting. The man had control, she had to hand it to him, and there was a part of her that wanted very much to snap it. She took a deep breath. What would happen if she just got out of her jeans and jumped him?

But there was another part of her that wanted even more to torture him the way that he'd been torturing her. That was the part she went with.

First, she had to get his T-shirt off. Drew lifted arms that felt like jelly, tugged his T-shirt out of his jeans and slid her hands beneath it. She gripped his waist the way that he had done, but her thumbs were about five inches apart. Following her own instincts, she closed the distance between them and began to move her hands slowly upward.

Within seconds any thought she'd had of one-upmanship faded because all she could think of was Kit. She'd known that he was beautiful, but it was quite another thing to experience that beauty up close. His skin was warm and smooth and faintly damp. Glancing up, she saw that his eyes were glittering now like black diamonds and his hands had fisted at his sides. The control was costing him, and she couldn't help feel some satisfaction. She shifted her attention back to his chest. His muscles felt like steel beneath that smooth skin, and she could feel them expand and relax as he breathed in and out. His chest hair was soft and silky, narrow at his waist and thicker, more luxuriant near his pecs.

Shoving his shirt up higher, she didn't object when he helped her pull it off of him. His shoulders were corded with muscles and his skin was a lovely golden shade of bronze. A Greek god was what he looked like and, for tonight, he was hers.

She began again, pressing her hands to his waist and drawing them up his broad chest. His nipples grew harder when she ran her thumbs over them. At the sign of his response, she shuddered. Just who was she torturing? she wondered.

She moved her thumbs over his nipples again, absorbed his quick intake of breath. "I just love your body. It's—" Then, because she simply couldn't resist, she leaned forward and tasted the nipple that had grown so hard beneath her thumb.

"Drew." His voice was husky, his breath rasping, as his hands gripped her head and pushed it away. "That wasn't in the lesson."

"You didn't like it?"

"I liked it…a lot, but we're not going to get through the rest of it if you keep that up. Much more and I'll take you right on the floor."

"Big talk." She traced one finger down the center of his chest and over his stomach, stopping only when it was blocked by the snap of his jeans. "I wouldn't have any objection to that. But—" lowering her other hand, she pulled the snap open "—let's wait a bit, shall we? I'm not through with you yet."

She slid her fingers beneath his waistband, just the way he had. His stomach muscles clenched. This was fun, she thought. She was enjoying torturing them both. What did that say about her? She pulled open the snap. The sound was loud and erotic in the quiet room.

She didn't have to look up to know that he was watching what she was doing. She could feel the heat of his gaze as she fumbled with the zipper. Then she tugged it down and pulled it apart just as he had done. No lace panties, but she found the black jockeys were an effective substitute—at least, for her.

"Nice," she said.

What she was about to do next had her drawing in a deep gulp of oxygen. Then she slid her hand beneath the elastic and wrapped her fingers around the long, hard length of him. His groan was the perfect echo of what she was feeling. But she wasn't done yet. She hooked her fingers in the elastic and pushed the cotton briefs down, freeing him. Then she dropped to her knees, took him into her mouth and stroked him with her tongue.

"Christ." Kit threaded his fingers into her hair. "Drew."

The plea in his tone sent pleasure arrowing through her.

"Stop." The word was a hoarse whisper as he gently, but firmly, pulled her mouth away.

"I'm not finished," she objected.

"I will be in a matter of seconds if you keep that up." He hoisted her to her feet. "You're full of surprises."

"I just did what you did."

"With a few improvisations," he muttered as he scooped her up and carried her into the bedroom.

"The thought of you taking me against the wall again turned me on. Not to mention the floor."

The heat of his glance seared her. "We'll get to both, I promise you. But right now, I'm thinking about protection." He laid her on the bed and opened a drawer in the nightstand.

Shock moved through her as she realized that she hadn't thought about it, not even once. But even that thought faded as she watched him tear open a foil package and sheath his erection. He was beautiful and she could feel the throbbing begin again just looking at him.

Then he was on the bed, drawing her legs apart and settling himself between them. He braced himself over her, filling her vision, her world.

"I can't wait any longer, Drew."

She wasn't going to complain. Not when she felt the urgent evidence of his desire pressing against her. She arched, taking just a little of him into her. Need sliced through her making her arch again. "More."

"Damn." In one smooth stroke, he thrust all the way into her.

"Yes. Yes!"

"Wrap your legs around me."

As soon as she did, he gripped her hands, linking her fingers with his. "Hold on. It's going to be a rough ride."

He began to move then, drawing out and pushing in, picking up the rhythm with each stroke. There was none of the gentleness he'd shown her when he'd touched her. She didn't miss it, not when she had this. As she moved with him, meeting each thrust, Drew felt her world narrow to this man and where he was taking her. The pulsing inside of her just built and built.

His voice was a rough rasp at her ear. "Come with me, Drew. I want you with me. Now."

Crying out Kit's name, she leapt with him.

14

KIT STRUGGLED to surface. Reality trickled into his mind in little spurts. He became aware that he was lying on top of Drew, crushing her. He had to move. But he couldn't, not yet, not until he caught his breath. What in hell had just happened? He'd intended to make love to her, to slowly restoke the fires that had built in both of them in the living room.

But the sight of her lying on his bed, naked, waiting for him, had snapped his control. He'd had to have her. What was she doing to him? He'd felt desire before—but it had always been reasonable, manageable.

When he tried to lever himself up, he realized that he was still trembling. "Are you all right?"

"I think so."

She sounded as winded as he did, so he rolled, taking her with him and shifting until she was lying on top, her legs tangled with his, her head nestled against his shoulder.

"I don't think I can move."

"I'm with you there." The fact was he didn't want to move. As he lay there, simply holding her, Kit felt something move through him—not desire and certainly not that blast of fire that had nearly consumed him moments before. This was something softer, warmer. He felt as if he could go on holding her this way for a very long time.

That was another first for him.

Drew lifted her head and met his eyes. "That was—" She paused, then continued, "I don't have a word for it, but it was even better than before."

"I'm with you there, too."

"And I want to do it again."

He tucked a curl behind her ear and was amazed that he managed a grin. Evidently, he'd recovered the use of his arm and face muscles. "Sure thing. But I need a little recovery time."

"But I can't."

Kit had an idea that he was losing the thread of the conversation. "You can't give me some time?"

"No, I didn't mean that. You can have a lot of time. But I…I don't think I should make love with you again."

"Why not? You just said you didn't have a word to describe it. I agreed with you. You said you wanted to do it again. I one hundred percent agreed with you. And if you're still having reservations about the quality of your technique, you did just fine. In fact, you're a stellar example of the student surpassing the teacher."

She frowned at him. "I'm serious. Making love again is not a good idea."

Kit reached up to smooth the little line that had formed on her forehead. "Aw, nuts. We were on a roll there, agreeing on everything, and now you've gone and messed it up. Are you forgetting that I promised we'd do it against the wall again?" He leaned down and feathered his lips over hers. "I'm a man of my word. And I think you also requested the floor."

"No, I didn't. And stop kissing me. You know where that's going to lead." Drew pressed her hands against his shoulder and shoved. "I'm serious about this."

Kit smiled at her. "I can see that. So why don't you explain to me why you don't want to make love with me again?"

"I do. I told you that. But I'm not being fair to you."

Shifting her off him, he rose from the bed and discarded the condom. He extracted another one from the dresser, then took her hand and pulled her from the bed. "Why don't you explain it all to me while we take a shower?"

She narrowed her eyes. "You're not going to need that condom."

"I believe in practicing safe sex, don't you?"

"Of course I do. But I'm trying to explain to you why we shouldn't make love again."

Reaching into the shower, Kit placed the foil packet in the soap dish and twisted the faucets. "Go ahead. Explain."

"Because I'd be using you."

"I have no objection to that." He dropped his gaze. "And it looks as though I don't need any more recovery time."

Drew couldn't resist following the direction of his gaze, nor could she do anything to fight off the sudden wave of heat that shot through her at the sight of his erection. He was definitely ready. The melting and throbbing sensations inside of her told her that she was ready, too.

Except she wasn't. Lifting her gaze to his, she tried to ignore what she was feeling.

"You're thinking about it, too," he murmured. "You're wondering if it could possibly be as good as the last few times."

"Stop that right now." She fisted her free hand on her hip. "I'm trying to explain to you why this isn't a good idea."

"Okay. I'm all ears."

She drew in a deep breath. "When you came back here, I told you that I'd changed my mind about kissing you again because I wanted to live in the moment."

Kit kept his eyes on hers as he tested the shower spray and adjusted the faucets. "I see. Seize the day. Gather ye rosebuds while ye may—that kind of thing?"

"Yes. Exactly."

"I can sympathize with that. I've had more than my fair share of 'seize the day' moments, believe me. So what's the problem?"

She frowned at him. "Don't you get it? I was just using you for escape. And that's not fair. I should…we should be thinking about what to do next. I can't stay here hiding. I…we have to find out who I am and who was shooting at me."

"Is that all that's bothering you?" Kit lifted her into the shower with him. She sputtered when the spray hit her full in the face, and by the time she'd shoved her hair out of her eyes, he'd lathered his hands and was rubbing them over her shoulders and up her throat.

"Yes, but…" His fingers were gentle and distracting as they traced first her cheekbones and then her jawline.

"I don't see a problem. First, I think it's very sweet that you have such a strict conscience and that you're concerned about me. Two qualities that are not the hallmarks of a criminal mind, by the way. Second, I enjoyed having you use me." He glided slick palms down her arms and up again.

"In fact, I'll give you carte blanche to use me anytime you want. And if it will make you feel less guilty—" he slid his hands down her back "—I'll use you right back."

He was doing it again, Drew realized, emptying her mind and sweeping her into a world where only sensations existed. Even the sound of his voice seemed to ripple over her skin, making her more sensually aware of him.

"As far as thinking about what to do next, I have a few ideas—but sometimes taking a break from the problem can stimulate my brain cells."

She hadn't felt his hands move, but suddenly they were at her waist, drawing her closer so she could feel the hard press of his erection against her stomach. Then they slid over her buttocks and he slipped his fingers between her legs and into her folds. In one deft movement, they parted her and found her heat. She closed her legs trapping them there.

Leaning down, he drew an earlobe between his teeth and nipped it.

A tremor moved through her. "You're not being fair."

"Hey, you were worried that *you* weren't being fair. Turnabout's fair play. I'm just trying to even the score."

She felt herself tighten around his fingers as they moved inside of her. The orgasm came out of nowhere and it slammed into her with the speed and power of a Mack truck. The shock waves were still reverberating through her when his hands gripped her buttocks and lifted her. It was a good thing he did, or she was sure she would have melted onto the floor of the shower.

"Wrap your pretty legs around me, Drew."

She did as he pressed her back against the wall of the shower. The soft hair on his stomach rubbed against her clitoris and the hard length of his penis slid between her cheeks. She hadn't thought it possible, but more ripples of heat coursed through her.

"Now open your eyes. I want you to watch what I'm doing."

What strength she had left Drew channeled into opening

her eyes. And it was worth the effort. With water cascading over his hair and down his face and shoulders, he reminded her of some ancient god who'd just walked out of the sea to claim her.

Raising one hand, he reached for the foil packet and tore it open with his teeth. Then he pulled the condom out. She found even those movements erotic. But the word took on new meaning when he moved his hands beneath her butt and began to slowly work himself into the latex. A flash fire moved through her as each movement rubbed him roughly against her. She was practically panting for him by the time he grasped her hips again.

She waited, aching for his thrust, needing to be filled by him, but all he did was press her more firmly against the wall. He was there—right where her body was craving him. But he still didn't enter her. She tried to arch her hips, but she couldn't move. "Please. Now."

"Look at me, Drew."

When she met his eyes, Kit said, "All the senses, remember? I want you to watch me enter you."

She would have done anything he asked. Anything. And the sight of him pushing into her slowly sent new shock waves of pleasure through her. She felt her inner muscles tighten around him, soften and then tighten again. "Do it again."

He did. But he was still too slow, still not deep enough. Desperate, she tried to increase the pace, but he wouldn't allow it. Instead, he shifted closer, his fingers digging into her hips.

"Look at me now, Drew."

She did, and the glittering hunger in his eyes had her contracting around him. She tried to move then, gripping his shoulders, determined to ride him and put an end to the torture. But he shifted his hands to her buttocks and began to lift and lower her at his pace, not hers. At the end of each thrust, heat built with such intensity that she was afraid she might implode at any second. And still he continued those sure, slow strokes. Each time she neared completion, he sensed it and withdrew. Then he started all over again, rebuilding that exquisite tension inside of her. It was heaven. It was torture. And she wanted more.

Just one more time. Kit could feel his climax building with each heartbeat, just waiting to thunder through him, but he had to enter her just one more time. With each thrust, those green eyes went dark and then blind with pleasure. Pleasure that he wanted to continue giving her. And each time he buried himself inside her, he felt the ripples of her contractions pull him impossibly deeper. He was losing parts of himself here, but he couldn't stop. His world had narrowed to this moment, this woman, and he couldn't control what he was feeling. All he knew was that he had to have more.

Even as the first pulse of his release ripped through him, he tried to hold back. He might have succeeded if her nails hadn't dug into his shoulders and he hadn't felt her climax begin to radiate through her in slow convulsions. His mind went blank and, pressing her against the wall, he began to drive into her fast and hard until sensation consumed them both.

15

WHILE SHE ROLLED UP the sleeves of the shirt he'd given her to wear, Drew watched Kit pull items out of the grocery bag that Cass had brought and line them in a neat row on the counter. He was dressed in black jeans and a San Francisco 49ers T-shirt. And he was still barefoot.

Just looking at him had her own bare toes curling against the floor. Get a grip, she warned herself, and forced her eyes back to his face.

"Perfect. Aunt Cass knows what I like. One of the benefits of having a psychic in the family." As he spoke, he pulled a skillet from a rack hanging overhead and in a series of economical moves located a bowl and utensils. "How do you feel about Greek omelets?"

"Guilty. You don't have to cook for me. Some crackers to go with that cheese would be fine."

He grinned at her. "In the Angelis family, that would be pathetic. We believe in feeding our guests." He handed her a glass of wine. "Sit down. Feel at home. I enjoy cooking and omelets are one of my specialties."

Drew slid onto a stool. The problem was she did feel at home and it was making her nervous. Being here in the kitchen with Kit and watching him cook was somehow just as intimate as making love with him. She liked being with him, and the feeling was somehow…familiar.

The kitchen was small but neat and efficient. The sink and cook top were built into the island. The appliances were stainless steel, the cupboards sleek and glossy and the color of granite. This room, like the rest of his apartment, had an essentially masculine feel to it. So why would it feel familiar? She had a hunch it wasn't her surroundings that were making her feel this way. It was the man.

And she had no business feeling at home with him. Not when she didn't know who she was or what she'd done. Drew took a quick sip of her wine. "Is there anything I can do to help you?"

Kit glanced up. "Not at the moment." After selecting an onion from a wire basket, he peeled the skin off and began to dice it with quick, skillful strokes of his knife.

"You're good at this," she said.

"I should be." He scraped the chopped onions from the cutting board into butter that was bubbling in the skillet. Then he sliced tomatoes in half and removed the seeds. "I was practically raised in the kitchen of The Poseidon."

"Did your Mom work there, too?"

"No. She had her hands full raising the four of us. Then she and my Uncle Demetrius died in a boating accident when I was ten. Theo and Nik were eleven and twelve and Philly was only four."

Drew reached across the counter and closed her hand around his wrist. "I'm sorry. That must have been hard."

He captured her fingers and gave them a squeeze before releasing them. "It was. It was hard for my aunt Cass, too. Her son, Dino, was twelve, my brother Nik's age. My grandfather insisted that my dad and Aunt Cass and all of us move back here, and Aunt Cass shouldered the lion's share of taking care of five kids, aged twelve to four. Then, as her psychic consultation business grew, we'd all go to the restaurant after school instead of here, and Dad, in self-defense, put us to work. I found out early that I liked working in the kitchen better than bussing tables and scrubbing floors."

"But you didn't go into the restaurant business."

He met her eyes, and she could see a trace of regret in his. "No. I disappointed my father. We all did. There's still a chance that Dino will come back after his stint in the Navy and take over the restaurant, but right now our cousin's got a bad case of wanderlust."

"Being part of a big family sounds like fun."

Kit smiled as he broke eggs into a bowl. "Fun if you like chaos and hard work. But we had breaks. When we were little, Dad would close the restaurant on Sundays and take us fishing at Granddad's cabin or to a ball game. Philly and Aunt Cass would do stuff like visit museums, go to the symphony and ballet, girl things."

Her eyebrows shot up. "The symphony and the ballet are girl things?"

Kit shrugged. "Give any man a choice between the ballet and a baseball game and what do you think he'll choose?"

"Point taken."

Kit extended his hand. "Tell you what, if you'll go to a ball game with me, I'll go to a ballet with you. Deal?"

Drew glanced at his hand, but she didn't take it. "Maybe I hate the ballet."

"Then the Fates are being kind to me. But I know you'll love baseball. I mean, what's not to love? Shake my hand."

She stared at him. "You can't be serious. When we find out who I am, what I did, you may never want to see me again. We can't make plans like that."

He moved around the counter and took both her hands in his. His eyes were very serious. "If that's what's got that worry line on your forehead, you can relax. This isn't some kind of a one-night stand for me, Drew. No matter what we find out, I'm going to want to see you again. I'm going to want you in my bed again—not to mention my shower."

She couldn't have explained what his words meant to her, how the warmth of them and the promise soothed away all the tension that had been building inside of her since she'd walked into the kitchen.

Releasing her hands, Kit extended his again. "I'm warning you that this may be your only chance to get me to a ballet. So is it a deal or not?"

Her lips curved as she grasped his hand in hers. "Deal."

"Now that we've settled that, we'll deal with what else is on your mind—what we're going to do tomorrow." Turning his attention back to the cook top, he flipped the tomatoes and onions with a deft movement of his wrist. "From what I've observed about you so far, you're a woman who likes to look before she leaps. So you'll need a plan."

Something in his tone had her chin lifting. "I will?"

"Sugar, when we find your purse, I'll bet you a home-cooked meal that there'll be all kinds of organizational tools in it, including a PalmPilot with your daily engagements."

Drew couldn't explain why she felt a bit annoyed at the description.

Kit poured eggs into the pan and began to stir them.

"Speaking of your purse, I'm wondering what exactly happened to it. It wasn't at the church. If you'd left it there, Nik would have found it and bagged it. And you didn't have it in the taxi."

"No. I looked for it."

He glanced up at her. "I'm thinking there's a possibility that it fell into someone else's hands."

She frowned. "The man I shot?"

"Could be. I'm particularly thinking about those two men in the van. If they'd gotten hold of your purse, they might have been hanging around the church hoping that you would come back for it. One of them could have been the man you shot. I've been running scenarios through my mind. In one of them, after you shoot this guy, he backs out of the room just as Roman reaches the top of the stairs. They struggle. In the meantime, you and the bride and groom leave by the back stairs and exit the church through the sacristy. In your hurry to leave, you forget your purse. Of course, it's just a guess."

Drew met his eyes. "If they have my purse, they must know my name and my address."

"That's a possibility we'll have to consider when you remember who you are."

The way he said the words as if it were a certainty sent a ribbon of warmth through her. Kit tilted the pan and continued to stir the eggs. There was a competence about the way he did it—a competence that seemed to carry over into everything he did.

"You're the expert at investigating a case," she said. "What do you suggest?"

"Usually, I start by reviewing just the facts." He crumbled cheese over the eggs. "Why don't you start? Summarize what we know so far."

She thought for a minute. "I woke up in a taxi with a bump on my head, a wedding dress in a bag, a tote with a recently fired gun and twenty-thousand dollars in cash. I was dressed in a fairly expensive suit and shoes, and I had no memory of who I was, where I was coming from or where I was going. There was blood on my suit—not mine." She paused to consider, then added, "I had your card, and I learned from the taxi driver where he'd picked me up—on Bellevue."

Kit gathered plates, utensils and napkins out of cupboards and drawers. "Excellent. You'd make a good investigator. Continue."

"In your office, I recalled holding a gun and pulling the trigger at a large figure I'm sure was a man. You learned from your brother that there'd been an interrupted wedding at St. Peter's Church, which was on Bellevue and Skylar and that your friend Roman had been hurt."

"And, when I got there, I discovered that a man had been killed in the sacristy. He had a gun in his hand that had been fired. Roman had been overheard arguing and probably fighting—most likely with the groom."

"Just the facts," Drew reminded him.

"Touché." He shot her a grin as he cut the omelet in half and slipped it onto two plates. "Even though the caterer didn't see the fight, it makes sense that it was Roman and the bridegroom. Shots were fired. Later, Roman fell over the railing of the choir loft. There was a gun in his hand that also had been fired." He set a plate in front of her. "I just learned from Nik that the dead man in the sacristy was Gino DeLucca, Paulo's bodyguard, and the bullet that killed him most likely came from Roman's gun."

"If Roman shot that man, it must have been in self-defense," she said firmly.

"I agree, but that's theory." He sat down next to her and picked up his fork. "We're sticking to facts. I discovered more evidence of shootings in the loft storeroom—blood on two different walls. I saw the wedding bouquet the bride left behind. And earlier I saw a purse that belongs to Sadie Oliver. So she must have been there, too. Since her cell's in her purse, I haven't been able to reach her. Neither has her father. Can you think of anything else?"

She shook her head as she cut into her omelet and took a bite. For a moment, Drew was distracted by the explosion of flavors on her tongue. "This is good."

"Thanks." Kit lifted his wine and took a sip. "There are a lot of facts we don't know."

She nodded as she scooped up another bite. "I agree. We don't know for sure why Roman was there, who I am, why I was there, why Sadie was there, how Roman fell, where the bride and groom are. And how did so many people get wind of a secret wedding at the last minute?"

"Good question."

For a moment they ate in silence. Then Kit said, "Now what the police are doing is creating a scenario that fits the facts that they do know. In their minds, Roman came to stop his sister's wedding. They'll probably figure that's why Sadie was there, too. I'm thinking there were at least two other men with guns at the church—besides the body-guard. There was the one you shot and the one the caterer saw shoot Father Mike. The police will believe that Roman brought some help along to get the job done."

"But you know better."

Kit set down his fork. "I know it didn't happen that way.

I know Roman almost as well as I know my brothers. I've seen the way he is with his sisters."

Drew slipped her hand into his as he turned to face her. For the first time, she glimpsed how the trouble his friend was in was tearing him up inside.

"I keep thinking of what I would have done if it was Philly getting married last night to a man I thought was all wrong for her. Would I have tried to talk her out of it? Absolutely. Would I go there with guns to shoot everyone?"

"No," she said. "And neither would Roman."

"How can you be so sure of that? You don't know Roman."

She smiled at him. "I know you, and he's your friend."

He leaned forward and kissed her softly on the mouth. "You're very sweet."

When he drew back, neither of them spoke for a moment. Then she asked, "What's your scenario?"

"Roman came to the church to talk his sister and Paulo out of going through with the wedding. But he wasn't the only one who came to put a stop to the nuptials. There were at least two other men, maybe more. I figure these guys are probably not expecting Roman. So the shooting starts, and perhaps the bodyguard gets caught in the crossfire. Paulo runs to the choir loft to protect the bride. I'm thinking that since he brought his bodyguard to the wedding, he might have been carrying a gun, too—just in case. And let's say another guy follows Paulo upstairs and Roman takes off after him. After all, his sister is in that upstairs room. I figure the guy Roman is following goes into the storeroom."

"And he's the one I shot?"

"Could be."

"Why didn't Paulo shoot him?"

Kit met her eyes. "Good question. Maybe he couldn't.

Could be he's wounded from the shots that were fired in the sacristy. That would explain the two areas of blood in that storeroom."

"So Paulo gives me his gun and I shoot one of the bad guys."

"But you don't kill him—he stumbles back out of the storeroom, struggles with Roman and they tumble down the stairs. In the meantime, the caterer distracts the shooter who's trying to kill Father Mike. She runs and hides, dials 9-1-1. While that's going on, you and the bride and groom make tracks. That's my best-case scenario. In my other one, you escape and some of the bad guys snatch the bride and groom—and maybe Sadie Oliver, too."

"You're worried about her."

He nodded. "I can understand why the bride and groom might decide to hide out for a while, but if Sadie could, I think she'd be in that hospital with Roman."

"Yes." Drew frowned as she thought about it. "So two bad guys escaped."

"At least two. The one you shot and the one who shot Father Mike. But they left witnesses. You, for one, and the caterer, for another."

"Don't forget Roman. He could be in danger."

"There's a policeman posted at his door."

Drew looked down and was surprised to find that her plate was empty. Sliding off the stool she carried it to the sink. "Now that we've looked at the facts and the dueling scenarios, what's next?"

Kit joined her and transferred plates and utensils to the dishwasher. "We go back to the facts and pick out the ones that are odd, that don't seem to fit either scenario."

"The whole thing is pretty odd," she said.

"I'm with you there."

She swallowed the last sip of wine and handed him the glass. "Not the secret wedding. That's understandable because of the feud between the families. But usually couples who get secretly married elope."

"It's harder to elope when you're Catholic, so religion may have played a role," Kit said.

"But it's harder to keep a secret wedding secret if you hold it in a church and hire a caterer."

"Agreed. Roman and Sadie and you clearly knew about the wedding. So did Paulo's bodyguard. What else strikes you as odd?"

"The money. What in the world was someone doing with twenty-thousand dollars?"

Kit took her hand and led her into the living room. "Maybe it belonged to the bride and groom. Could be they were planning on eloping *after* the wedding." He pressed a button on the stereo and the sound of a low sax spilled into the room. "Paulo would know that credit cards could be traced."

"You're good at this," Drew said. "I never thought of that."

"Practice." He pulled her into his arms and began to dance.

"Is dancing part of your regular routine when you're going over odd facts?" she asked.

He drew her closer and turned her in a circle. "I'm improvising. But don't let me interrupt your train of thought. What else seems odd?"

"Your card. How did I end up with it? And why did someone give it to me?"

"I was wondering when you'd get to that." Kit turned her again, and she stopped resisting the urge to lean her head against his shoulder. "I figure you either got it from Roman or Juliana."

"But why?"

"Whoever it was wanted you to get help—to come to me and tell me what had happened."

"Which I wasn't able to do—and now your friend is the prime suspect in all of this."

Stopping, he framed her face with his hands. "That's not your fault. You came to me and I am helping and we're going to get to the bottom of this." He trailed his hands down her arms and up again, then drew her close. "So to summarize, the odd details are—the bride and groom didn't elope. But the tote full of money isn't so odd if it was getaway cash, and neither is the fact that you had my card and flagged a taxi to bring you to my office."

"What is odd is that I ended up with the money."

"Agreed. Maybe after you contacted me, we were supposed to use it in some way. They had no way of knowing you were going to be in an accident and lose your memory."

"They could be waiting for us right now."

He pulled her closer when she tried to draw away. "You're going to remember." Then suddenly he stopped dancing. "It's also odd that you ended up with the wedding dress. Why wasn't the bride wearing it? Or why didn't she at least take it with her?"

They both glanced to where the dress bag was laying across the back of a leather couch. Then Kit continued, "You know, you haven't parted with that since this whole thing began. You wouldn't leave it at my office or at the restaurant."

Sliding his hand down her arm, he drew her with him to the couch. "Do you want to do the honors?"

Drew nodded. Her heart was beating fast as she un-zipped the bag and carefully lifted the dress out. "Look at the bead work. This is all done by hand. This dress must have cost a small fortune."

The dizziness hit her the moment she ran her hands over the tiny pearls that were sewn into the lace. The same piano music was playing, the same scene floated on the air, and she saw the young couple she'd seen before holding hands and staring at a mannequin that was wearing a beaded dress. She could make out other things—glass cases filled with scarves, more dresses hanging from indi-vidual racks. Then the young woman turned to her and said, "We love it."

Drew felt something like joy move through her and then the image abruptly faded. When she opened her eyes, she saw that she was sitting on the couch with the dress draped across her lap, and Kit was seated on the glass-topped coffee table, holding her hands.

"What did you remember?" he asked.

"It was a shop. You were right about that. They came into a shop and they liked this dress. Not the wedding dress, but it had the same kind of bead work. Loved it. And I felt wonderful. Maybe I sold it to them. The dress must have been expensive. All those pearls are sewn in by hand."

"I've got an even better theory." Releasing her hands, Kit carefully picked up the dress and showed her the label.

"*Designs by Drew.* I'm betting you created it."

16

"This is the third store," Kit said. They'd arrived at Pier 39 in the Fisherman's Wharf area at eleven and begun threading their way through the levels crowded with tourists. The sun was pouring down and glinting off the water in the bay. Before that, they'd stopped at the hospital and learned that Roman was in surgery. Drew had wanted him to stay at St. Jude's, but he couldn't ignore the feeling that they were very close to discovering who Drew was.

"MsFit," Drew said. "Nice name, but I don't recognize it."

Because he could see the tension in her shoulders and feel the nerves radiating off of her, Kit ran a hand down her arm from shoulder to wrist. "Look in the window and see if anything looks even vaguely familiar."

"This is like looking for a needle in a haystack," she complained, but she did what he asked.

Kit could understand why she was a bit discouraged. So was he. The excitement they'd felt when they'd discovered the label in the wedding dress had faded when they hadn't been able to find a listing for Designs by Drew in either the white or the yellow pages, or even one hit on the Internet.

Just a minor setback, he'd assured her. They just had to find the shop that she'd remembered. Together they'd scoured the phone book, making a list of department stores, specialty boutiques and dress shops that carried high-end items. "We've got a plan," he'd said as he'd carried her off to bed.

In the morning light, he realized that the task was a daunting one. His best hunch was that they would find their needle in a haystack here in the pier area because they'd been close to it when Drew had had that memory flash. Plus, the back of his neck had been tingling ever since they'd arrived.

"See anything?" he asked.

"No. The customer here is older. Look at the dresses. They're very matronly. This isn't a shop that a young couple would have come into."

"You don't want to go in?"

She met his eyes squarely. "No. I'm not going to give you an opportunity to buy anything else for me."

He took her hand as he studied the store map. "Okay. The last store is on the top level. It's called Prestige Designs."

"You're not buying me anything else there, either."

"Okay."

Drew sent him a sideways glance as he guided her up the stairs. "You say that, but I don't trust you. If we go in, something will catch your eye just like it did in the first two stores. Men aren't supposed to like to shop."

"Is that like the 'real men don't eat quiche' thing?"

"Yes."

"You agreed that you needed clothes, so I bought you some."

She held up a finger. "Clothes, yes. One outfit. That

was the plan and that's what I agreed to. I didn't need the other things."

It hadn't taken her long to select the sundress and the strappy sandals, and she'd worn the entire ensemble out of the first store with the clothes she'd borrowed from Philly neatly folded in a shopping bag over her arm. She might not remember who she was yet, but she hadn't forgotten her sense of style. He doubted that she wore anything quite as plain as Philly's jeans and T-shirt even on a casual Friday.

"I told you. I bought the hat and the sunglasses because I don't want you to be too recognizable. Our friends in the van are still looking for you, and they may have your purse. While it's highly unlikely they'd be here, I'd like us to be prepared." He checked his mall map and then spotted the sign he was looking for. "And you agreed."

"To the hat and the sunglasses," she said as they stopped in front of a display window. "But I didn't need earrings and the scarf."

He flicked the cascade of gold circles dangling from one of her ears. "They were gifts. If you don't like them, you can always take them back."

She frowned, fingering the scarf that she'd tied around her waist. "I like them. You know I do. I was practically drooling over the earrings, and the scarf adds just the right touch to this outfit. But they weren't necessary."

Unable to resist, he drew his finger along her jawline. "My practical Drew."

She let out a huff of breath. "Maybe I am practical. One of us has to be. These are not inexpensive shops. And I don't even know if I'll be able to pay you back for the clothes."

"I'll be happy to extend you credit over time. I'll even offer you my five-year plan at an all-time low percentage rate."

She fisted her hands on her hips, but Kit saw her lips twitch. "You are an impossible man to argue with."

"I do my best." He slipped an arm around her and turned her toward the display window of Prestige Designs. "Let's just look in the window."

She did as he asked, studying each item on display with that total concentration that was so characteristic of her. While she did, he dialed St. Jude's hospital and learned that Roman was still in surgery. He would be all right, Kit assured himself.

As if she could tell exactly what he was thinking, Drew slipped her hand into his. Then she suddenly went rigid. Quickly, he scanned the items in the shop window. One headless mannequin wore a pair of long silky pants with a sequined top. Another wore a white gauzy, three-tiered skirt with an embroidered shirt. Kit felt the prickling sensation at the back of his neck.

"It's the shirt, isn't it?" he asked. "I'll bet the pieces you design all have something fancy like that—embroidery, beads. It's probably your signature."

"I'm not sure." She pressed a hand against her stomach. "I didn't feel anything when I first looked at it, but my eyes just keep going back to it."

"Let's go in and get a closer look." He took her hand in his and drew her through the glass doors of the shop.

IT WAS ALL DREW could do not to dig in her heels when she heard the music. Piano music. The flowery, cloying scent was there, too, and she realized that it was coming from a display of bottles on a glass-topped counter. The sign read *Flair,* Prestige Design's signature scent.

"I'm right here." Kit squeezed her hand.

Despite his denials about being psychic, she was beginning to think that the man could read her mind. Sweeping her gaze around the interior of the store, she took in the mannequins, the individual racks that showcased one or two dresses.

"This is the place," she whispered.

"Yeah, I figured that with the music and that horrible perfume. You okay?"

Drew nodded.

A young woman, a pert redhead in a black skirt, white blouse and sensible heeled pumps, hurried toward them. "Drew." She gave Kit an appreciative once-over before she continued in a hushed voice. "Be careful. The Dragon Lady is very upset that you didn't come to work last night. And you're late this morning." She glanced at Kit again. "But I don't blame you a bit."

"Miss?" A well-coiffed woman in an orchid pantsuit had the young woman glancing over her shoulder. "I'll be right there." Before scurrying away, she spoke to Drew again. "Good luck with Dragon Lady."

"I don't recognize her," Drew said.

Kit squeezed her hand. "You will."

Slacks and tops were artfully arranged on a table to their left. To their right was a second glass-topped counter with jewelry. But it was what was at the back of the store that caught Drew's eye. Hanging from one of the racks was a slim sheath trimmed with lace and seed pearls that were an exact match to the wedding dress. Drew ran her hands over the intricate work. Kit slipped the hanger off the hook, but she was sure even before she saw the label what it would say. *Designs by Drew.*

"Lovely, isn't it? One of our very talented staff designed it."

The voice had Drew jumping guiltily and turning.

The woman stood ramrod straight, her steel-gray hair pulled back into a ballerina knot. A pair of wire-framed glasses perched low on her nose. She wore the black skirt and white blouse that seemed to be the sales consultants' uniform. Her lipstick matched the crimson polish on her carefully manicured nails, and the initial smile on her face morphed into a disapproving frown.

"Drew? Is that you?"

Drew nodded, taking her sunglasses and hat off. But for the life of her she couldn't think of anything to say. This had to be the woman the redhead had called Dragon Lady.

"Well, I'm surprised that you have the nerve to show up here." She glanced at her watch, "You failed to arrive for work yesterday, and you were due in two hours ago this morning. Actions have consequences, young lady. I'm afraid that you no longer—"

"I insisted that Drew come to see you," Kit said. "I'm Nate Cashman, by the way. Drew's agent. And you're…"

Drew stared at Kit as the Dragon Lady gave him a once-over.

"I'm Cordelia Whitlaw. You're her agent, you say?"

Kit beamed a smile at her. "She signed on with me yesterday." He pulled a card out of his pocket and handed it to her. "Am I the luckiest man in the world or what?"

The Dragon Lady glanced at the card and then back at Kit. "And you're representing her for…"

"Perhaps we could discuss this in a more private place?"

Kit leaned closer and spoke in a low tone. "People are beginning to stare."

Drew glanced around and saw that staff members and customers were indeed sending curious glances in their direction.

"Follow me." Dragon Lady whirled to lead the way through a nearby door.

"What are you doing?" Drew protested as they followed Cordelia through a storeroom and into a small, neatly appointed office.

"Just play along with me. The D.L. needs to be shaken up just a bit."

D.L.? Drew had to swallow a sudden urge to laugh. This wasn't funny, she told herself. "The D.L...." She pressed her free hand against her stomach to prevent a giggle from escaping. This woman, her boss, was going to fire her, and that wasn't a laughing matter.

Kit nudged her into one of the chairs facing the desk and settled himself in the other.

Cordelia Whitlaw shifted a small box from a filing cabinet to her desk. Then she took her chair and folded her hands in front of her. "When you didn't show up for work last night, I cleaned out your locker. I did warn you that if you continued to ask for time off, I would have to terminate our agreement. And your absence last night after I specifically told you that I needed you here by six and not a minute later..." She spread her hands. "Well, you had to have known the consequences."

Drew felt as if she'd been dragged into the principal's office. Had that been a frequent experience for her? she wondered.

"And just what was your agreement with Drew?" Kit

pulled the box closer, lifted the cover and began to rifle through the contents.

"She knows quite well," the D.L. said with a sniff. "When she first brought me her designs, I said that I would be quite happy to carry them on consignment."

Kit's glanced up from the box. "What's the split?"

"The store gets eighty percent and she gets twenty along with a job." The D.L. shifted her stern gaze to Drew. "As part of our arrangement, she was to work on weekends and holidays until the money from the sales of her designs began to come in on a regular basis. Ordinarily, I don't do that, but I made an exception in this case. And she failed to live up to her end of the agreement."

"May I see the contract?" Kit extended his hand.

"Contract?" For the first time since they'd entered the office, the woman's stiff composure slipped just a little. "I...we didn't draw anything formal up."

"I see. That's very good news for us. Drew told me, but I couldn't believe that she was selling her designs without a contract."

"I don't want you to get the wrong impression," the D.L. said. "We're very happy with Drew's designs. We want to continue to carry them in the store."

"That may be a problem," Kit said. "Neiman Marcus is interested in carrying her designs, but they want exclusivity."

"Neiman Marcus?"

"I've had a nibble from Bergdorf Goodman, too." He glanced at his watch. "We're doing lunch with their head buyer. Can't be late."

"No. No, of course not." She turned to Drew. "Surely we can come to some arrangement. After all, this is where you first made a sale. We wouldn't want to lose you."

Kit glanced at Drew. "It's up to you."

Drew rose. "I'll have Nate talk to Neiman Marcus. They may make an exception for a small boutique."

"But she'd want her job back," Kit said. "Temporarily, of course. And more flexible hours. I'll spell it all out in the contract."

"Of course."

Kit put the lid on the box containing Drew's belongings and tucked it under his arm. Then he grabbed Drew by the hand and urged her out of the office. "You'll be hearing from me, Ms. Whitlaw. Ta."

LAUGHING AND BREATHLESS, Drew nearly tripped when Kit came to a sudden halt on the sidewalk and raised his hand to flag a taxi. "I can't believe you did that. And you couldn't have planned it. I mean, you couldn't have known that you would have to…that she would be so…"

"Insufferable?"

"Yes. She was awful. I could barely keep from laughing when you called her 'D.L.'"

"Short for Dragon Lady. An apt name." A taxi picked up a fare in the other side of the intersection. Kit shifted the box under his arm and raised his hand again. "The old biddy needed to be taken down a notch."

"She did. But where did you…how did you come up with that business card? And Nate Cashman? Where in the world did you come up with that name?"

Satisfied that an empty taxi was headed their way, Kit turned to her and, for a split second, he lost his train of thought. There was something about seeing her laughing up at him in the sunlight. She'd never looked at him in quite that way before, and something twisted in his heart. Before he could even think, he pulled her close and covered her mouth with his.

He'd been imagining doing that all during the time she'd shopped for clothes. He'd been starving for the sweet, dark richness of her taste. He'd even imagined joining her in one of the dressing rooms for a quick kiss. But he didn't entirely trust his ability to control himself where she was concerned.

Shoppers and tourists streamed by, parting to move around them. In some part of his mind, he was aware of the muffled laughter, but not even a strident wolf whistle motivated him to stop. More than anything, he wanted to pull her closer, to feel the softness of her breasts and thighs pressed against him. To touch her, really touch her. In a moment, he would.

"Hey, buddy! You might want to take this taxi before someone steals it from you."

Drawing back, Kit glanced over his shoulder to see a plump woman, holding several packages.

She winked at him. "It'll give you a little more privacy, too."

He grinned at her. "Good idea. Thanks for holding it for me."

"The Poseidon restaurant," he said to the taxi driver as he climbed in beside Drew. To the question in her eyes he said, "We're going to grab a bite to eat. Now where were we—you wanted to know about Nate Cashman. If memory serves me, I found old Nate in the phone book. But I've also picked up some good ones in the credits of movies— you know, where they list everyone who ever delivered a package to the set. I use those to find names for characters in my books, too."

"And the card you just whipped out of your shirt?"

"I carry a few with me at all times. Nate's is especially useful. Part of being a good P.I. is being able to lie quickly and well at a moment's notice. And you picked up your cues like a pro."

"It was fun. I suppose I should feel guilty about that, but this is one time when paying the piper will almost be worth it."

Kit's expression sobered. "What do you mean about paying the piper? You've got your job back."

"But once Ms. Whitlaw finds out the truth, that you're not my agent and that Neiman Marcus doesn't want my designs exclusively, she'll fire me again."

"She most certainly won't." He winked at her. "Not while you've got Nate Cashman on your side." Taking out his cell phone, he punched numbers in.

"Who are you calling?"

"My brother Theo. He's the man who writes up all my contracts. I'm not sure he's picking up his cell. I'll just leave him one more message."

Theo answered on the second ring. "This better be important."

It was only when his brother spoke that Kit realized how much he'd wanted to hear that soft drawl.

"I'm pulling into the parking lot at St. Joe's right now," Theo continued.

"Then Mario contacted you?" Kit asked. "You're taking Roman's case?"

"He hasn't been charged yet. I'm hoping it won't come to that."

For the first time since he'd stood next to Nik staring down at the tape that had outlined Roman's body, Kit felt some of his concern for his friend ease. Now that

Theo was on the scene, he knew that Roman was in good hands.

"If that's why you called to leave me one more message..." Theo began.

"I also need a favor."

"Of course," Theo drawled. "Why else would you call?"

The dry note in his brother's voice had Kit's lips curving. "I could mention that turnabout's fair play. I've done my fair share of pro bono work for you."

"Make it fast. I'm in the elevator on the way up to Roman's floor."

"I need a contract drawn up—a client of mine has a verbal agreement with a shop on Pier 39. They take her designs on consignment and give her twenty percent when and if something sells. I think a fifty-fifty split would be more equitable. And if they balk at that, I'd like a second contract to stipulate that if they want the designs, they have to buy them up front at a price to be negotiated and agreed to by the store and the designer."

"Got it," Theo said. "I'll add that the selling price has to be negotiated, too, and that if it's raised, the designer has to be compensated at fifty percent of the increase."

"I like the way your mind works, bro. Hold on for a second, will you?" Leaning forward, Kit spoke to the driver. "Go right on past the front of the restaurant, and drop us off at the alley entrance."

"You won't get anything from me until Monday or Tuesday at the earliest," Theo said. "I'll have my new intern handle it."

"You have an intern?"

"Just got myself one. Is that all you wanted?"

"Keep me posted," Kit said.

"Ditto."

As the taxi braked to a stop in the alley behind The Poseidon, Kit closed his cell and put it in his pocket. "Theo's at the hospital."

"Do you want to go there?" Drew asked.

Kit let out a frustrated breath. "Roman's still in surgery. I'm of more use to him if I can find out what really happened in that church."

"You will. You're going to find the truth."

The belief in her eyes did a lot to soothe the anxiety moving through him. He passed a bill to the taxi driver and then drew her out of the car. "We're going to find the truth together—if you're up to it."

"What do you mean?"

"I have a plan."

17

THE POSEIDON WAS packed. Philly had squeezed them into a table near the bar where customers stood two deep. Waiters deftly threaded their way through the crowds, their trays piled high with food, and the scents were making Drew's mouth water.

Above the buzz of conversation and the clink of dishware, Drew could just catch the thrum of Greek music. It drifted in from the outside patio where she caught a glimpse of a dance floor. Kit had elbowed his way to the bar to fetch some wine, and she could see that he was talking to his father as he watched the latest newscast on one of the TVs hanging from the ceiling. Glancing at the screen, she recognized the front of St. Peter's Church. But she couldn't catch what the newscaster was saying. The next shot was of two young people. Beneath the photos were the names—Paulo Carlucci and Juliana Oliver.

Her head swam for a minute as she recognized the couple from her dream. She once again pictured them in her mind as they pushed through the glass doors of the shop she now knew as Prestige Designs, and she felt the joy they'd radiated. The love.

Another face flashed onto the TV screen, a handsome man. The caption read Roman Oliver.

The memory flashed into her mind, making her head spin. Fighting against the terror that was flooding through her, she pressed her hands to her temples to keep the images in focus. Roman standing at the top of the choir loft stairs, a gun in his hand. She felt the weight of a gun in her own hand.

"Juliana? Are you all right?" a male voice cried out.

"Yes."

The answering voice—also male—came from behind her. Before she could turn her head, another man leapt out of the darkness and grabbed Roman. He was huge, built like a tank. Blood stained his T-shirt and ran down his arm. The two men fought, ramming into the railing and the wall, their bodies pressed so close together that might have been lovers. Fear coiled into an icy ball in her stomach as they teetered for a moment on the balcony railing. She was sure they were going to fall to the floor below. Then they were on the balcony floor, and Roman was on top.

"Roman!" Someone rushed past her.

"Get her out of here, Paulo. Go to Kit Angelis and—"

The last word was a strangled sound. Then as quickly as the memory had come, it vanished. Drew found herself trembling, staring at Kit, who now had his cell phone pressed to his ear. He'd be checking on Roman. And he'd been right about his friend. Roman *had* tried to protect Paulo and his sister. Just as Kit was trying to protect her.

Her gaze shifted to the box that the Dragon Lady had emptied her locker into. Kit had placed it on the table, but she hadn't worked up the courage to open it. Instinct told her that in the quick search he'd done in the D.L.'s office, he'd discovered something that he hadn't told her yet. Now he was giving her time to make her decision.

She known him less that twenty-four hours, and yet she felt like she'd known him forever. He was a good man. Smart and funny. Generous and sweet. A combination of guardian angel and warrior. A man who trusted his instincts and wasn't afraid to take a risk. And though she had no right to, she was on the brink of falling in love with him.

Panic sprinted through her. She absolutely couldn't let herself do that. It wasn't fair to him. And allowing him to go on shielding her wasn't fair, either.

She nearly jumped when Helena dropped into the chair across from hers. "Welcome back. I see that Kit is remembering how he was raised and he's feeding you this time."

"Yes."

"The food here is very good, but I will be offended if Kit doesn't bring you back to my place upstairs tonight. Then afterward you can come down here and dance some traditional Greek dances."

Today, Helena wore a thin cotton blouse in a vibrant red color and white slacks. Gold hoops glinted at her ears. Then Drew noticed the motorcycle helmet she'd tucked under her arm and her eyes widened.

"Don't tell me. You actually bought a motorcycle?"

Helena lifted a key, letting it dangle from her thumb and forefinger. "I took the morning off and spent the time becoming the proud new owner of a Harley. That was the easy part. It is trickier learning how to ride it. But I've ridden smaller ones in Greece."

She glanced at the bar. "I've never been one to let the grass grow under my feet. Until I met Spiro. So I think you were right. It's time I unbalanced the status quo."

Drew leaned closer. "Does Spiro know about the bike?"

With a quick grin, Helena leaned closer. "He's about to

get the news. I'm going to invite him to go for a ride with me tonight after work. You'll have a ringside seat if there are fireworks."

She rose just as Kit returned to the table.

"Good luck, Helena."

Helena drew in a deep breath. "Here goes."

"What was that about?" Kit asked as he handed her a menu and a glass of wine.

"She bought a motorcycle and she's going to invite your father to go bike riding after work."

"Interesting." Kit glanced at the bar and then back to her. "You like to stir things up, don't you?"

She took a sip of her wine and set it down. "I don't know. After meeting Cordelia Whitlaw and hearing 'Nate Cashman' talk to your brother Theo about that contract, I'm beginning to think that I used to be the female version of Casper Milquetoast."

Kit angled his head as he looked at her. "Yet you had the guts to shoot someone in that storeroom."

"I'm not proud of that."

He picked up her hand and played with her fingers. "Maybe you should be. From what we've been able to gather so far, desperate measures were called for. I'm thinking that you're more like the heroine of *The Terminator.* Given the opportunity, you rise to the occasion."

Recalling her earlier resolve, she met his eyes. "I'd like to think so. Some of your theories are turning into facts."

His eyes narrowed immediately. "You remembered more. Tell me."

"I recognized Paulo and Juliana's pictures on the TV screen. They're the young couple that came into Prestige Designs."

"Anything else?"

She glanced down at the box on the table between them. "Before I tell you the rest, I want to know what you spotted in the stuff the D.L. cleared out of my locker. I can handle it."

He squeezed her hand. "I know you can. But, first, we order."

Though her appetite had faded, she scanned the menu. "What do you recommend?"

"Everything. My personal favorite is the lamb souvlaki."

"And souvlaki is?"

"A shish kabob without the vegetables. But you can't go wrong with gyro, which is a Greek-style hero sandwich with grilled lamb, tomatoes, onions and the house's special cucumber sauce." He sent her a quick grin. "Of course, if you want to live on the wild side, you could try the grilled octopus. It's the house specialty."

"I think I'm basically conservative. I'll take the gyro."

He signaled the waitress and ordered two gyros. Then he opened the box that he'd brought from the Dragon Lady's office. "You can examine everything, but the most important thing is the card." He handed it to her.

She stared down at her name. Drew Merriweather. In the lower left hand corner was *Designs by Drew.*

And an address—2355 Chelsea Street, 1A. She stared again at the name and concentrated hard. Drew Merriweather. That's who she was. She had no doubt of that. Surely, knowing the name should unlock…something.

Finally, she glanced back up at Kit. "Nothing. I'm not even getting a dizzy spell." The panic she'd been holding at bay broke through in such a rush that she shivered. "What if I don't ever remember?"

He took her hand again. "You will. I told you I have a plan. We're going to go there. But first, I had to arrange some precautions. Since your purse is missing, I'm still worried that those thugs who chased us last night may know who you are and where you live. So I made a phone call at the bar, and asked a pal of mine to help us out. Luke Rossi. He's a fellow P.I. who specializes in security. He's a real whiz kid when it comes to technology, but now and again, he has a yen to get out of the office and do a little field work. Right now, he's over at 2355 Chelsea, getting the lay of the land. If someone is watching the place, he'll spot them, and then we'll work around them. He's meeting us here in an hour. In the meantime, we're going to eat and build up our strength."

Drew took a sip of her wine. She didn't like it at all that Kit was putting himself in danger again for her. "What if that doesn't work? Nothing came back to me in the store. I may not remember anything when I visit my…" She wasn't sure what to call it.

"It's either your home or your place of business. Probably your home since you don't have a separate listing for *Designs by Drew*. And even if you don't remember anything, we'll find clues. And then we'll follow them."

She swallowed the panic and thought about being fair. He'd helped her from the get go—in spite of the blood on her suit, the recently fired gun and the money. She met his eyes steadily. "Look, you've been really great. But now that we know my address, maybe it's time that I went to the police. They can take it from here."

His eyes narrowed. "Don't you trust me to help you?"

"Yes. Of course, I do, but…"

"Then, I think we ought to go to the address on the card and see what we find."

She drew in a deep breath. "No. I want my twenty-dollar bill back. I'm going to terminate your services."

His eyes narrowed, and she caught a glimpse of steel. "I didn't think that you were a quitter."

Temper surged through her. "Your best friend is close to being arrested. One of the reasons for that is the police don't have the full story. While you were at the bar, I just remembered more. Paulo and Juliana were alive when Roman fell down the stairs. He came up to the choir loft to protect them."

"Tell me everything you remembered."

She did, then said, "So you see Roman must have struggled with the man that I shot. He told Paulo to take Juliana and run. He said to go to you. The police need to know that Roman was trying to protect his sister and Paulo."

"I agree."

"Oh." Drew felt as if the bottom of her stomach had just dropped out. He agreed with her. And that's what she'd wanted, right? Or had she been counting on Kit to argue with her and talk her out of going to the police? Was she that much of a Casper Milquetoast?

A waitress set platters in front of each of them. "Anything else?" she asked.

Kit smiled at her. "Not right now." Then his eyes returned to hers. "Eat up, and be sure to try the fries while they're hot. Dad makes them Greek-style with oregano and feta cheese. You squeeze the lemon wedge over them."

Drew glanced down at her plate, but she'd lost her appetite. Kit obviously hadn't. She watched as he lifted the gyro and took a bite. She cleared her throat. "If it's all the same to you, I'd like to turn myself over to the police right now."

"You're not turning yourself over to the police."

"But you just said you agreed that I should—"

"I said that I agree the police should know what you just remembered…eventually. But we've got a little time to play with. I'm pretty sure they won't charge Roman until he comes out of surgery and they can talk with him. Theo will know just how long he can stall the police. Meanwhile, I think the best plan is to see if we can jog your memory back into place. You may remember enough to clear Roman entirely."

A disturbance at the bar had them both turning their heads. They stared as Spiro lifted Helena off of a bar stool, tossed her over his shoulder as if she were a featherweight and carried her through the door behind the bar. Applause broke out along with a few cheers.

"Well, I'll be damned," Kit said. Then he returned his gaze to Drew. "You are a very dangerous woman."

"DID I JUST SEE what I think I saw?"

Kit glanced up to see Nik and the redheaded caterer, J. C. Riley, approaching their table. What in the world was his brother doing here? "You did, and my friend here, Drew Merriweather, is the instigator. She encouraged Helena to buy a motorcycle."

"Helena bought a motorcycle?" Nik grinned down at Drew. "Good job. It's high time one of them made a move. Drew, this is J. C. Riley."

J.C. extended her hand to Drew. "How do you feel about sharing? That food looks wonderful, and I'm fainting on my feet."

"Sure," Drew said. "Help yourself. I'll never eat all of this."

As he offered his chair to J.C., Kit deftly lifted his own plate and said, "Enjoy, ladies. Nik and I have a little business to talk over."

J.C. popped a Greek fry into her mouth with one hand, and waved them away with the other.

"Not very subtle, bro," Nik commented as Kit nudged him out of earshot and toward the bar.

"What are you doing here? You said you were going to find a way to continue working on the case."

Nik signaled the bartender for a beer, then grabbed a fry from Kit's plate. "I might ask the same of you. I thought you were working on the case, too."

"I am." And it wasn't going well, Kit thought. Drew was thinking of bolting. He could have handled her having second thoughts about the situation she was in, but his gut told him that she was thinking of bolting from him, too. As he watched her laugh at something J.C. said and then squeeze lemon over a fry, he realized that he wasn't going to let her walk out of his life.

"And the blonde is helping you out?"

"She's a client."

"Nice-looking."

Kit frowned at his brother. "She's taken."

Nik grabbed another fry. "Nothing like mixing business with pleasure, I always say."

"It's not like that. Is that what you're doing with the caterer? Mixing business with pleasure?"

Nik's eyes narrowed. "Watch it, baby bro. To borrow your words, it's not like that."

There was something in his brother's eyes that had Kit backing down. "Okay, what say we change the subject? I need the latest you've got on what happened at St. Peter's. The news channels have been running the same loops over and over again."

Nik took a sip of his beer. "You can't breathe a word."

Kit nodded.

"The two families have received ransom notes. Someone is holding the bride and groom hostage."

"Then Roman is off the hook?"

Nik shook his head. "Parker is favoring Roman for the kidnapping. Of course, he had to have had accomplices. There's an APB out on his sister Sadie right now."

"Sadie? They think she played a part in all of this? You've got to be kidding."

"She's disappeared. No one has seen her or talked to her since last night."

"And Roman ended up falling over a railing, getting a skull fracture and having to undergo spinal surgery because…"

Nik shrugged. "The best laid plans often run amok."

Kit let out a frustrated breath. "This whole thing is ridiculous. I couldn't even make this plot work in one of my books. Why would Roman and Sadie kidnap their own sister?"

"The line of reasoning is that they had to kidnap both the bride and the groom to divert suspicion from themselves."

"That's crap. What kind of motive is Parker giving Roman?"

"Money. The Olivers had to come up with a lot of money for that land deal on the Orange County coastline and…" Nik let his sentence fade away as he suddenly pointed to one of the TV screens.

Kit glanced up to see Carla Mitchell's face on the screen. Beneath her image were the words *Breaking News*. Kit immediately recognized the man standing to her left as Angelo Carlucci. The man was in his fifties and, though his hair was gray, he still looked fit. Carla introduced him and then let him speak into the microphone.

"Since the police aren't doing anything to get my son back, I'm addressing this plea to Mario Oliver. I know that we've been business rivals. I also know that your son is behind this terrible tragedy. He shot my son's bodyguard. But I don't care. Just give me my son back. Please." He passed the microphone back to Carla.

"Well, the shit is going to hit the fan now," Nik remarked. "I'll bet Commissioner Galvin is already on the phone to Parker."

On the screen, Carla was saying, "You heard it here first. Roman Oliver is a prime suspect in the murder of Paulo Carlucci's bodyguard and in the kidnapping of Paulo Carlucci."

"This is going to get very ugly if Roman is tried in the press," Nik said. "The D.A. will be under a lot of pressure now to charge Roman."

"Theo's going to have his hands full."

Nik glanced at him. "Theo's taking the case, then?"

Kit nodded. "He's at the hospital right now."

Nik put his hand on Kit's shoulder. "If I were in Roman's shoes right now, Theo's the man I'd want on my side."

"Yeah." Kit felt some of his tension ease. "You know, Drew pointed out something to me."

"Drew, the client?"

"Yeah. She said that for a secret wedding, this one wasn't much of a secret. If Roman and Sadie got wind of it, so could've some others. And I'm thinking maybe the bodyguard could have spread the word to someone else who had a reason for stirring up the hatred between the two families. Who would benefit from doing that?"

Nik snatched another Greek fry as he turned Kit's

theory over in his mind for a minute. "Nice scenario. J.C. was thinking the same thing last night. There is that big land deal that the two families are in competition for. Maybe someone wants their attention elsewhere. Stirring up a blood feud would do that nicely."

"If both families have to ante up big bucks to get back their kids, what happens to the land deal?"

"I like the way your mind works." Nik swatted Kit's hand away to steal another fry. "I'm going to give Cole Buchanan over at Rossi Investigations a call and have him do some research. He might as well earn the money the mayor is paying him to give me backup with J.C."

Kit glanced over at Drew and wished to hell that he could tell his brother what she'd remembered. It would go a long way in clearing Roman.

He listened to Nik leave a message for Cole Buchanan. Then together they brainstormed by running over the possible suspects again. He objected heatedly when Nik offered the theory that Sadie Oliver might have masterminded the whole plan either by herself or in partnership with Michael Dano. But he knew the value of considering even the most remote possibilities. And all the while, he kept checking to see what Drew was doing.

"You can't keep your eyes off that client of yours, can you?" Nik asked.

Kit looked back at his brother and knew immediately that he'd made a mistake. Nik had always seen too much. He watched as his brother shifted that very perceptive gaze to Drew.

"There's something you're not telling me and it has to do with Drew, doesn't it?"

"No...I—"

"Dammit." Nik looked at Drew again. "She's part of it, isn't she? She's the mystery blonde, the woman that J.C. saw come into the church with Juliana. And you haven't brought her to the station? What in hell are you thinking? You could lose your license for withholding evidence in a homicide."

As Nik slid from his chair, Kit grabbed his arm. "I'm not withholding evidence. Not yet. I…I need you to listen."

Nik stared at his brother for a moment, then nodded. "This had better be good."

J.C. WAVED A HAND in the direction of the bar. "They're about to get into a brawl."

Drew glanced over and saw the tension between the two men. Even at a distance, she could feel temper coming off them in waves. Guilt roiled in her stomach. She had a good idea what they were fighting about. She started to rise, but J.C. clamped a hand on her arm. "Leave them be. I have four brothers and they fight all the time. My stepmother boots them out of the house so that they don't break the furniture. Men." She lifted the half of the gyro that Drew had sliced off for her. "There's a basic genetic difference between them and us."

Drew kept her eyes on Kit, and only relaxed a bit when she saw Nik slide back up on his stool.

"Of course, there's the physical difference, too."

The smile in J.C.'s voice had Drew turning back.

"I can handle the physical difference. In fact, I enjoy handling it." She grinned at Drew, then jerked her head in the direction of the brothers. "They certainly are magnificent specimens, aren't they?"

"They're beautiful." The Angelis brothers were really something. Nik was a bit shorter than Kit, but there was a toughness emanating from him that made you forget that. He had the same classic features, made all the more attractive because his nose was a bit crooked. Her stomach settled a little as the two brothers continued to talk without either of them throwing a punch. "The first time I saw Kit he reminded me of a fallen angel."

"Good description. The first time I saw Nik, I thought of Adonis, the mortal man who had two goddesses fighting over him."

"They're certainly something to fight over."

"You should have some of this gyro," J.C. said around a mouthful of food. "It's excellent. I really have to get the recipe."

Absently, Drew picked up a fry. If Kit had told his brother who she was, it was only a matter of time before Nik came over to arrest her. Unless…Kit talked him out of it. Narrowing her eyes, Drew decided that was exactly what was going on right now. "But Kit is not an angel."

"Neither is Nik."

"Kit's a stubborn, determined man," Drew said. "He pretends to listen, and then he just goes and does exactly what he wants."

J.C.'s eyebrows shot up. "I'd say it runs in the family." Then she grinned. "They must get it from their dad. Looks like he was about to get his way when we walked in."

"It's not fair. And I can't let him make every decision for me. I think…I'm afraid I'm the kind of a woman who does that—leans on a man, I mean."

J.C. lifted the wineglass and handed it to her. "You're afraid of that? Don't you know?"

Drew shook her head. "I can't remember anything about myself. I have amnesia."

J.C. almost spit out a mouthful of gyro. "Amnesia? Seriously? Like in the soaps? I can't imagine. Did you want to talk about it?"

Drew did, and they took turns sipping from the wineglass. J.C. only interrupted once to point a fry at her and say, "So you must be the mystery woman, the one I saw get out of the car with the bride."

"I guess. I can't remember anything. I just get flashes now and then."

J.C. squeezed her hand. "You'll remember."

"I have to turn myself in. People are following Kit because of me, and he could probably lose his license for not cooperating with the police."

J.C. handed her the wineglass. "You're sloppy in love with him, aren't you?"

Drew took a sip to quell the rising panic. "No. Of course not. And I'm not going to fall in love with him. He's... we're...that's not going to happen. It can't."

She glanced at Kit and then back at J.C. "I'm going to need your help." She pressed a hand against her heart to steady its rhythm. "All you have to do is keep Kit distracted for a few minutes. Tell him that I've gone to the ladies' room. Can you do that? Please?"

"If that's what you want." J.C. gave Drew two thumbs-up. "We witnesses have to stick together, don't we?"

18

DREW DIDN'T RUSH toward the ladies' room, but her mind was racing. Looking back to see if Kit was following her might give her away. The man had an uncanny knack for figuring out what she was going to do.

She glanced around as she entered a small hallway. There were three doors, one marked Men to her right, one marked Women to her left and another marked Exit. All three were in full view of the bar where Nik and Kit were sitting. So she had to go in the restroom. It was small—just one stall and a tiny vanity and mirror. Paper towels were stacked neatly in a brass basket and next to it was a vase of fresh violets. Pretty and welcoming, Drew thought, and then she spotted the window high overhead. Perfect.

Or almost. It was a good three feet in width, but maybe only a foot high. Since it opened outward on a crank, she'd have the entire height to wiggle through. She could do it. She climbed onto the vanity and carefully got to her feet. The window opened to the alley. Getting a good grip on the sill, she jumped up and got her chest on the window ledge. Then she twisted, wiggled and generally muscled herself through the opening until she was teetering half in and half out of the bathroom.

And she was stuck.

Drew tried to wiggle forward hoping to pitch onto the alley floor. No luck. Next she tried twisting this way and that. But she couldn't make progress. Finally, she tried wiggling backward, and that's when she heard the rip of silk. The scarf that Kit had bought for her was caught on something. She reached back to get a grip on it and her legs and her feet shot upward.

Enough of her weight had shifted forward so that it was her thighs that now rested on the window ledge. Her fingers were only about six inches from the ground but she couldn't quite reach it.

The sound of the restroom door opening had her taking in a fresh gulp of air. "Hey," she called, "can you give me a hand?"

"Be glad to."

Her stomach did a little flip. Then Kit's hands gripped her waist, and he yanked her out of the window. Two seconds later, she was facing him on the bathroom floor. The room was even smaller than she'd thought, and Kit seemed to take up most of it.

He was angry. She'd never seen him this angry before. And he was standing so close. She couldn't even take a breath without inhaling his scent.

Something tangled in her stomach, something that had heat licking along her nerve endings. She took a quick step back and hit the stall door. When she stepped to the side, he slapped his hand against the wall to cage her in. Heat flicked through her again. She slipped her hands behind her back so that she wouldn't touch him.

"You're not going anywhere until we settle this, Drew."

She lifted her chin. "Okay. Fine. I'll go back to the table with you and we'll talk." But she had to get out of this room, or in a minute, she was going to jump him.

"I put an Out-of-Order sign on the door and I locked it. We're not leaving until you tell me why you're running away."

She narrowed her eyes. "I'm not running away. I'm going to the police to turn myself in. Nik wanted to take me in, didn't he? And you talked him out of it, didn't you?"

"You're no good to the police until you get your memory back. Going to your house might turn the trick."

"And it might not. Besides, the police can take me to the house. I don't need you for that."

The words were like a slap. But it wasn't the words so much as the fear they sent sprinting through him that had Kit grabbing her by the shoulders and pulling her against him. "You're not going to run away from me."

Maybe if she'd struggled, he'd have been able to pull back. Or perhaps if she'd surrendered, he'd have gotten some grip on his control. She did neither. Instead, her mouth was as demanding as his, her hands as desperate.

He pushed the strap of her sundress over her shoulders and down her arms. He hadn't planned to do this. But the sight of her in the window, the knowledge that in another few minutes she'd have been gone, out on the streets alone, except for two killers who wanted her dead....

He dragged his mouth from hers and tried to catch his breath. Gripping her shoulders, he shoved her up against the stall door. He wanted to shake her. He wanted to haul her to the floor. "Don't you know they could be watching this place? My car is still here. They'll figure that sooner or later, I'll come back for it. That's why I had the taxi drop us off in the alley."

She poked one finger into his chest. "They're shooting

at you, too. That's why I tried to leave. If I'm not with you, you're safe."

Understanding mixed with some of the fear still ruling him. "Let me handle the safety issue." When she hesitated, he said, "Haven't I done a pretty good job so far?"

"Yes, but…"

He gave her shoulders a little shake. "Well, I don't quit in the middle of something. You hired me, and I intend to finish this job. Tell me you won't pull another stunt like this."

"All right. I won't. Now, tell me that you're going to finish what you just started."

This time it was delight that shot through him. "Right here?"

"Right now." Wrapping her arms around him, she pulled his mouth down to hers.

Hunger built just as rapidly as it had a few moments before. Heat arrowed through him making him just as desperate. He slid his hand beneath her skirt to find her skin—soft, hot and smooth. He moved his hand higher, over her hip to her waist. Each separate response—the way her stomach muscles clenched, the little sound she made in her throat—tore through Kit and drove him to demand more.

He might have done something this reckless before, but not in years—and he'd never wanted anyone this much. Desire pounded at him as he dropped to his knees and dragged her panties down her legs, pulling sandals off in the process. Then shoving her skirt out of the way, he spread his fingers over her buttocks, drew her close and began to use his mouth on her.

The shock, an electric current, sizzled through her and sent her heartbeat racing. Drew let her head fall back and pressed her hands against the stall door for balance. She felt everything—the scrape of his teeth, the smooth, hard slide of his tongue, the pressure of those hard fingers branding her skin.

It was too much. It wasn't nearly enough. Each separate thrill drove her higher and higher until the climax poured through her in one searing wave.

Before she could ride it fully to its crest, he eased her to the floor and cradled her across his thighs until he'd dealt with the condom. She'd barely had time to reorient herself before he lifted her by the hips and shifted her so he was kneeling and she was straddling his lap.

"Wrap your legs around me."

Once she did, he filled her in a smooth hard stroke. For one blinding moment, the pleasure was so acute, she couldn't think, couldn't breathe. She simply closed her eyes and absorbed. Then desire tore through her again, and she tried to move, but couldn't.

"Look at me, Drew."

He held her still until they were eye to eye, then said, "Make me come."

The intensity of the hunger in his eyes had her inner muscles tightening around him deep inside of her.

A moan escaped his lips. "More," he breathed.

His hands imprisoned her and the most she could do was inch her hips up and down. Each time she did, pleasure rippled through her, but it wasn't enough for either of them. Layer after layer of tension built, but release was just out of reach. She'd never known this kind of torture, this kind of ecstasy.

Finally, she leaned forward, nipped on his bottom lip and breathed, "Let me finish this. Please."

"We'll finish it together, partner. Deal?"

She leveled her eyes on his. "Deal."

He released her then, and, finally free to move, she began to position her hips against him as surge after surge of pleasure slammed into her. She would have screamed if she could. But she was helpless to do anything but give herself to him.

Kit watched her through slitted eyes, moving just enough to drive her higher. He would have done anything to keep her here, thinking only of him and the satisfaction that he could give her. But in the same way that he was driving her, she was driving him, and finally, helpless, he had no choice but to surrender himself to her and to the completion that only she could provide.

Afterward, Drew broke the silence. "Well. I can't help but wonder if this is another first for me."

He found the strength to open his eyes and found that she was lying on top of him and they were stretched out on the floor.

"I know it can't be a first for you," she continued.

"And you know that because…" He was surprised to find his voice was working.

"You must have known right where that Out-of-Order sign was. Very smooth. I suspect that you and your brothers did a lot more in this restaurant than cook or bus tables."

Deciding that his best response to that was to change the subject, Kit tucked a finger under her chin. "You'll stick with me now?"

"Like glue. Until I get my memory back."

It wasn't the answer he'd hoped for. But he'd gotten part of what he wanted, and he knew how to be patient for the rest. He brushed her lips with his. "We have to get out of here."

She sat up. "I lost more of my clothes than you did."

He sent her a quick grin as she tugged her panties on. "We can always remedy that the next time."

She met his eyes. "Count on it."

19

"I GET THE FLORIST van, do all the scouting around and all you want me to do now is wait here for you?"

Chagrined. That was the best word Drew could come up with to describe the look on Luke Rossi's face. Luke was tall, with brownish blond hair and he wore glasses. She might have described the man himself as a computer nerd, if it weren't for the fact that he had the sleekly muscled body of a swimmer and the same kind of stillness about him that a jungle cat would have.

"Someone has to play lookout," Kit explained.

The van that had chased them the night before was parked half a block up and around the corner, where it had a good view of both the front and the back of the apartment building.

"If the van moves, if you see anyone get out, call me on my cell," Kit said. "And watch out for yourself. If they get suspicious about this delivery, they'll try to get by you."

Kit opened the door, Drew followed him out of the backseat and they circled to the rear of the florist van. After opening the door, he pulled out a potted palm and handed it to her. "Can you manage it?"

"Sure." It was heavier than she'd expected, but it covered her face and the entrance to her apartment building was only a few yards away. Once Kit had retrieved his palm tree, she followed him to the front door, where he punched the manager's button.

"Yeah?"

"Delivery for 1A. There's no answer, but I got a signature says I can leave it outside her door."

The buzzer sounded and Kit opened the door, waiting so she could precede him into the building. "The security here sucks," he commented.

Her heart kicked up a little as she moved down the hall. According to Luke, there were six apartments in all at 2355 Chelsea, and hers, 1A, boasted a little patio and garden. Kit would have preferred to come in that way, but the position of the van prevented it. At the end of the short hall, Drew stopped, and sure enough, there it was—right where Luke had said. 1A. She stared at the number and the letter on the door.

"You can put the plant down," Kit said, taking it from her. "We're going to leave them here. Ready?"

At her nod, he pulled out a thin tool and inserted it into the lock. "Let's hope that you don't have a security system. An alarm could cut our visit very short. Not only will the manager be displeased, but the goons in that van will probably join us."

She watched his hands, the long tapered fingers plying the pick with the concentration and precision of a surgeon. All the while, he was still rambling on about how she really ought to invest in a good security system and how Luke's firm, Rossi Investigations, could help her. He was doing it to soothe her nerves, Drew realized. And it was working.

She wondered if she would ever meet another man who would understand her quite as well as Kit Angelis did.

Maybe he was right, and she *was* like the heroine of *The Terminator*. Whatever was behind that door, whatever she remembered, she would rise to the occasion.

"We're in." Kit withdrew the tool, slipped it back into his pocket, then drew out a gun.

Her throat went dry as she stared at it. Had he been wearing it all day—even in the restroom?

"Remember the plan. I want you to stay to the right of the door until I scope the place out."

She knew the plan. He'd recited it to her twice on the ride over. If, by some chance, there was someone in the apartment, Kit would take care of them. But if anything happened to him, she was to run to Luke.

When she nodded and pressed her back to the wall, he opened the door, crouched and aimed his gun. Then he was gone. Fear shot through her. What she'd experienced a few minutes ago, worrying about what she'd discover when she regained her memory, couldn't hold a candle to what she was feeling now. Kit was risking his life, he was—

"It's clear."

Relief made her knees weak.

Kit reappeared in the doorway and took her hand. "It's not pretty."

It wasn't. Drew swept her gaze over the room, taking in the destruction. A few larger pieces of furniture, she could identify—an overturned sofa, a sewing machine lying on its side, what looked to be an antique desk, its legs sticking up in a dead-dog position. A bolt of lace had been unrolled and tossed into a heap in one corner, and near the door to the little garden, a floor lamp with a fancy fringed shade tilted drunkenly against the wall.

And over it all, like a blanket of newly fallen snow, lay unwound spools of thread in a myriad of colors—and beads, pearls, rhinestones and millions of sequins. She had an urge to laugh—or to cry—she wasn't certain which. She could even make out broken picture frames and pieces of torn photographs. Whatever had been here that might have triggered a flicker of memory was gone.

Kit drew her forward. "There are only two rooms." They circled the sofa and he led her through an archway into a kitchen. Sunshine streamed through the window, shining a harsh spotlight on the rubble strewn counters and floors. Food mixed with dirt and the remnants of dying plants.

"Anything?" Kit asked.

"It makes me feel sad, but I don't feel a personal connection to any of it."

"You will, soon enough." He turned to her then, and she saw that hint of steel in his eyes again. "And I'm going to get the bastards who did this. You can count on it."

Kit felt the tingle at the back of his neck at the same moment that he felt his cell phone vibrate in his pocket. Digging it out, he urged Drew toward the garden door.

"One's going around back," Luke said. "I'll handle the one at the front door."

Luke hadn't even finished his sentence when Kit spotted a man the size of a tank vaulting over the decorative picket fence enclosing the garden area. "Dammit. They've boxed us in."

Whirling, he pushed Drew back into the kitchen. "Climb out through the window." It was big enough, and with both men occupied, she could get away. If there were only two of them. "Don't think. Just run like hell." He handed her his cell phone. "Once you're clear of the place, dial 9-1-1."

The sound of splintering wood and glass had him racing back into the living room. He raised the gun, but not in time to stop the 300-pound tank who dove into his midsection.

The gun flew from his hand, discharging and skidding over debris as he and his opponent tumbled backward. Pain sang through every muscle, bone, and sinew in his body, but he rolled away as his opponent leapt onto the spot he'd just vacated and struck his head against the floor.

Okay, Kit thought, scrambling to his feet, brawn but not too many brains. He should be able to take him. Regaining his balance, he waited for the man to charge and managed to land a two-footed kick to his stomach. It barely slowed him down. Kit dodged a fist and grabbed a table leg off the floor before the tank charged again and slammed them both against the wall.

Hands the size of hams gripped Kit's neck. His vision blurred, then grayed. But he caught a motion. Someone was standing in the archway to the kitchen.

Drew?

Fear fueled the adrenaline already streaming through him, and he brought his knee up hard into the tank's crotch. The instant the fingers around his throat loosened, he shoved with all his might. His opponent stumbled backward but didn't go down. Kit cocked the table leg he'd picked up and swung. He heard the satisfying crunch of bone and the tank finally toppled.

He turned then and blinked. His eyes had to be deceiving him. Drew was standing in the archway, both hands gripping the gun—and she was aiming it at him.

"I won't shoot," she said in a shaky voice. "I just can't

seem to move my arms." During those endless moments when Kit and the other man had been locked in that deadly battle, she could have fired the gun. She would have if she could have been sure what she was seeing.

Memory hurt. She thought she'd feel relief, but it had been pain she'd experienced when the door to her past had suddenly opened. It had happened when she'd picked the gun up from the floor and brought her other hand to it just the way that Paulo had shown her in that dark room in the choir loft.

Paulo had put the gun in her hand that night and told her how to hold it, how to pull the trigger. Because he couldn't. He'd been shot in the arm.

That one memory had opened the floodgates, and the images in her mind had shifted from one to the other so swiftly that she couldn't distinguish between what had happened that night in the storeroom and what was happening right in front of her eyes.

Kit limped toward her, and it was only then that she believed he was all right. When he reached her, he covered her hands. "Just relax. That's it. That's it."

Drew felt the weapon slip from her hands into his, and then she sagged against him. His arms encircled her and a moment later she was sitting on the floor cradled in his lap. "I remember," she said. "I think I remember everything."

"Kit? You all right?" Luke's voice came from the hallway.

"Yeah," Kit called to him, "we're both all right."

She would be, Drew thought. As long as he went on holding her, she would be.

Luke shoved a handcuffed man into the room. He had a slighter frame than the felled giant, but he still could have played linebacker for the 49ers. And there was blood staining the bandage that wrapped his shoulder.

Kit dug a set of handcuffs out of his pocket and tossed them at his friend. "Good work."

"I might say the same." Luke knelt and slipped the cuffs on the giant. "This guy's a real bruiser. Mine has a shoulder wound, and it slowed him down some. He may be the one Drew shot."

"He is," Drew said. "I remember him now."

Sirens blared in the distance, and Luke added, "I called it in." Then he turned back to look at them. "I guess it worked. She got her memory back?"

"Yes," Drew said. "I remember everything. I have a family. My mom and dad live in Maryland right outside D.C." She could picture her dad lowering his newspaper to comment on something she and her sister were arguing about. "And I have a sister. She's Philly's age, finishing her senior year at Dartmouth." She was babbling, but she couldn't seem to stop. "And I live here—" she paused to glance around "—because I wanted to get away from them—from my parents. It's why I chose Stanford instead of a school back east. I wanted to be on my own. Mom and Dad would have helped me, financed my business, bought me a store, but I wanted to do it on my own." She tightened her arms around Kit's neck. "I know who I am. What I'm like."

The sirens had stopped at some point during her little recitation, Drew realized. There were footsteps in the hall.

"I remember what happened that night in the choir loft."

"Back here," Luke called into the hallway. "Everything is under control."

"Told you so." Kit managed to give her a quick hard kiss before the cops came in with their guns drawn.

20

KIT PACED BACK AND FORTH in a narrow five-by-ten room in front of a double-glass window. Through it, he could see Drew being interrogated by Captain D. C. Parker.

"You all right?"

He turned as Nik entered the room. "You should see the other guys."

"I did. You look worse."

"Thanks," Kit said. A brother always told you the truth.

"I also talked with Luke Rossi. He said you had a close call."

Kit shrugged. He didn't want to think about the fact that he'd very nearly lost Drew. "Is one of those bruisers the guy J.C. saw shoot Father Mike?"

No." Nik shook his head, a grim expression on his face. "She's working on a sketch of him with a police artist. Then maybe we can nail his ass, too."

"How much trouble am I in with your captain?"

"You mean for interfering in a police investigation by harboring a material witness? Parker should have thrown you in a holding cell and be threatening to revoke your license. Instead, he's allowed you to watch him interrogate the witness. That's pretty much red-carpet treatment."

Kit shifted his gaze to the window. Drew was sitting

there at a table, her hands folded, her knuckles white. "I want to be in there with her."

"You shouldn't even be in here. Hell, I'm not supposed to be in here. J.C. told me to come and check on you."

"Mind if I join the party?"

Both brothers turned to watch Theo amble into the room with coffee cups in a paper tray. "I brought coffee, the real stuff, not the sludge they serve here."

Nik elbowed his brother. "What do you think? You know what they say about Greeks bearing gifts."

"Ouch." Theo spoke, but both he and Kit winced.

Kit reached for a cup. It never ceased to amaze him that Theo could look elegant even in the most casual of clothes. Nik and he were both wearing jeans, but the seams weren't pressed the way Theo's were. All three of them wore summer-weight sport coats, but Nik's and his never seemed to fit the way Theo's did. It was little wonder in Kit's mind that it was Theo who'd made the most eligible bachelor's list. The man had a way of looking as if he'd just stepped off the cover of *G.Q.* "I thought you were at the hospital."

"I was." Theo eased a hip onto the long table that nearly filled the small room. "But Nik called me about your little adventure, and I thought I'd deliver some good news in person. Roman's out of surgery. The doctors were able to relieve the swelling at the base of his spine, and they're quite optimistic that there'll be no permanent damage."

Kit felt the pressure in his chest ease. How long had it been there, he wondered. "He'll beat you at tennis again."

Nik snorted, nearly spilling his coffee.

Theo merely raised one eyebrow. "I hope to prevent that."

"Hope springs eternal," Nik commented. Then he placed a hand on Theo's shoulder. "Good to have you here, bro."

"It's partly a working visit. I told my intern he could use Dinah's desk to make some calls."

"Sure," Nik said.

Kit glanced at the desk he knew to be Dinah's and saw the back of a dark-haired slender man who looked to be as well turned-out as Theo. "Have you been able to talk to Roman yet?"

"The doctors are keeping him sedated."

Nik gave a snort. "They won't get away with that excuse for much longer."

"I'll take every minute I can get," Theo said. "I've got a feeling that there's more bad news to come."

"Shit," Nik said.

Kit felt his stomach clench. Theo's "feelings" were as almost on the money as his aunt Cass's. And it only confirmed his own feeling that there was still another shoe to drop.

"As soon as Parker's done in there, I'm going to see what he'll tell me," Theo said, "and then I'm going to lean on an old friend at the D.A.'s office."

Nik grinned at him. "Good to know you're on the job." He jerked his head toward the glass. "While you're waiting on Parker, you'll get to hear the wedding-dress designer's version of what went on at St. Peter's."

Kit shifted his attention back to the room where D. C. Parker was just pressing down a button on a tape recorder. "I don't see why he has to keep going over it."

"It's standard interrogation procedure to take someone over their story several times," Theo said.

"To see if it changes or if something new emerges," Kit replied. "I know."

"Or to get a sense of whether or not they're telling the truth," Nik added.

Kit whirled on Nik. "She's telling the truth. I don't think Drew could tell a lie if she tried."

Nik raised his hand. "Easy. I'm not saying she's lying. But she fled from a crime scene with a gun that she admits firing and twenty-thousand dollars in cash."

"Paulo gave her the gun and the money. She's not a thief. She was supposed to give the cash to me and ask me to help them get away to safety somewhere. Have you gotten anything out of those two thugs we brought in yet?"

"The one J.C. shot is in the hospital, and he isn't saying anything yet. The other one has called for his lawyer and clammed up."

"I'd like to have just ten minutes with one of them."

Nik's eyebrows shot up as he shifted his gaze from Kit to Drew and back again. "She's more than a client to you."

Kit thrust a hand through his hair. "Yeah. You could say that. I'm in love with her. The forever kind of love, I think, and I don't know how the hell it happened."

At the expression on Nik's face, he set his coffee down, grabbed handfuls of Nik's shirt and pushed him into the wall. "If you laugh, I swear—"

"Hey." Theo grabbed his upper arms from behind. "You can't assault a cop in a squad room."

Kit dropped his hands. "I've got this feeling that she's not safe yet. Those two thugs were hired help. We still need to find out who's pulling the strings." His eyes narrowed. "Drew's testimony should at least force Parker to consider possibilities other than Roman."

"Look," Nik said, "if you want to help solve this thing, you might want to listen to her story one more time, yourself. Aren't you always saying that the clues are in the details?"

Kit met his brother's eyes. "I hate it when you're right."

Nik grinned. Placing a friendly hand on Kit's shoulder, he moved with him to the window. "You've always hated it. And I'm always right."

"Don't push your luck," Kit said as Theo joined them, and they all turned to watch the interrogation.

D. C. Parker was a tall man with a rangy build in his mid-thirties, with the kind of family connections and wealth that guaranteed he would become the commissioner of police one day. According to Nik, the captain was also a damn good cop, and the political part of his job was the part he liked the least.

"I'm going to ask you to repeat your story one more time, Ms. Merriweather. If anything new occurs to you as you go along, just add it right in. Any little detail that might occur to you might be of help."

Parker was being gentle with her. Kit had to give him points for that. But he could see the strain that telling the story over and over again was having on Drew.

"She's stronger than she looks," Nik commented.

"Yeah," Kit said, and then shut up as Drew began.

"I first met Juliana and Paulo when they came into Prestige Designs, a store on Pier 39 that carries my designs. Juliana was interested in the bead work I do, and we got to talking. She asked me if I would create a wedding dress for her. She offered me a very generous amount of money, but I couldn't let anyone know I was doing it, not even my boss. The wedding was a secret. No one could know. I agreed to make the dress and to keep the secret. They were so in love. So happy."

"And you had no idea who their families were, at first?" Parker asked.

"No. They didn't tell me their last names. They gave me cash to buy the materials for the dress, and Juliana came to my apartment for fittings. It was only as Juliana and I grew to become friends that she confided in me about the long-standing feud between their families. She'd promised Paulo that she wouldn't tell anyone in her family, and I think she needed another woman to talk to."

"And you didn't tell anyone about the secret wedding, what day it was or when it was taking place?"

Drew lifted her chin. "No. I told you that I didn't even know when or where the ceremony was going to take place until the afternoon that Juliana came to pick up the dress and she asked me to please come with her to the church. She wanted me to stand as a witness. More than that, she wanted a friend. So I called Prestige Designs to tell them that I wouldn't be in and I went with her."

"You got to St. Peter's shortly before seven," D.C. prompted.

In the observation room, Kit spoke softly to Nik and Theo. "She was at my office just after seven-thirty. Whatever happened went down fast."

"What did you do then?" Parker asked.

"Juliana and I entered through the back door of the church, the one next to the parking lot. And Juliana led me through the sacristy and up the back stairs to the choir loft."

"There was no one else in the sacristy when you walked through it?" Parker queried.

"No. Paulo and Father Mike were in the room on the other side of the altar. I spotted them, but Juliana didn't want Paulo to see her. Bad luck. So we went up the stairs and directly into the storeroom. I didn't even get a chance to take the wedding dress out of the bag when we heard angry voices quarreling. Then there were shots. Two." She paused to take a sip of water.

"That checks out with what J.C. heard," Nik commented. "Roman arrived, argued with Paulo to stop the wedding, then the gunfire started, and Roman shot DeLucca."

"I'm still saying that DeLucca pulled a gun and Roman killed him in self-defense," Kit said.

"Unfortunately, we don't have a witness to verify that," Theo commented.

At Kit's angry look, he continued, "I'm just telling it the way a good prosecutor's going to play it to a jury. The secret to building a good defense is to anticipate your opponent's moves."

Kit didn't comment this time. He was too intent on what Drew was saying. Nik had been right to tell him to listen again. Each time she repeated the story, the events became clearer in his mind.

"Juliana wanted to run out and see what had happened," Drew continued. "But I got to the door first and opened it just a crack. Paulo was running across the loft toward us. His shoulder was stained with blood. He was carrying a gun and the tote with the money. He gave both of them to me. Said he couldn't shoot and I'd have to use the gun. He told me how to release the safety and how to hold it."

While Drew took another sip of water, Nik said, "Dinah traced the serial number on the gun. It belongs to Paulo Carlucci."

In the interrogation room, Drew continued. "There was another shot. It was louder than the first two."

"That could have been from the man who shot Father Mike," Nik said. "J.C. calls him snake eyes."

"Then we heard footsteps. I looked and saw another man running up the stairs from the vestibule," Drew said. "He was big and he had a gun."

"What happened then?" Parker prompted Drew.

Kit could see that her knuckles were white, her back ramrod straight.

"Paulo shut off the lights and shoved Juliana in the corner. He stood in front of her. I kept the gun pointed at the door until it opened. And I shot the man who came through it. He stumbled back out. I couldn't see him anymore." She pressed a hand to her temple.

"Do you want to take a break, Ms. Merriweather?" D.C. asked.

"No. No, I want to finish this. I went to the door, and Roman shouted to his sister. 'Juliana, are you all right?' I could see him reach the top of the stairs. Behind me, Paulo said, 'Yes.' Then the man I shot leaped out at Roman. Roman told us to run, to go to Kit. Then we left."

"You ran along the choir loft and down the sacristy stairs?"

"Yes. We went out the side door and ran along Bellevue until we could hail a cab."

In the observation room, Kit shook his head. "Why in hell didn't Paulo and Juliana come with her? Something's going on here that we're not seeing yet." He turned to Nik. "What about Father Mike? Has he woken up yet?"

"Yeah," Theo said. "I talked to him at the hospital. He and Paulo were talking in the room on the other side of that altar. He says Paulo heard someone come into the sacristy and went to check it out. Then the shouting started and the shots were fired. The next thing he knew, someone hit him on the back of the head. When he came to and got to his feet, he ran into a man with a gun who was wearing a mask. He remembers J.C. throwing her cell, and then the gun went off. His memory's foggy after that."

In the interrogation room, Parker prompted Drew. "Then you ran—you and Paulo and Juliana."

Drew nodded. "We used the sacristy stairs and went out the side door."

"J.C. must have ducked into the closet by that time, and the man who shot Father Mike must have been checking out the rectory trying to find her," Nik theorized.

"The Fates were on the good guys' sides for a lot of this," Theo said.

In the interrogation room, Drew continued. "We went down an alley, and Paulo hailed a taxi. He told me to take the money and the gun to Kit and ask for help. That was the last I saw of Juliana and Paulo."

"You're sure?"

"Yes."

"Why didn't they get in the taxi with you?"

Drew shook her head. "I'm not sure. They were talking about that while I got myself into the cab, and I didn't catch all of it. But I think Paulo was worried. I don't think that he was willing to trust Roman's suggestion that we all go to Kit. They ended up telling me to call Juliana on her cell when Kit had come up with a plan. But then I got in the accident and—"

"Lost your memory," Parker finished for her. "And Juliana is not answering her cell. You have no idea where the bride and groom might be? They didn't tell you where they were going to wait for your call?"

"No. If I knew where they were, I'd tell you."

"I certainly hope so, Ms. Merriweather." D.C. Parker's tone had shifted from gentle to stern. "Wherever they are, they could be in mortal danger. Did Juliana tell you where they planned to honeymoon—anything like that?"

Drew shook her head. "She never said a word about that."

Kit watched as Parker handed her a card and told her to call him if she remembered anything, anything at all, and relief washed through Kit. "He's going to let her go."

A moment later, Parker joined them in the observation room. He nodded at Theo. "Good to see you, counselor. Then he shifted his gaze to Nik. "Taking a break, Detective?"

"Ms. Riley's in my office, sir, finishing up with the artist."

Parker jerked his head and Nik walked back into the squad room.

"I'm Roman Oliver's attorney," Theo said. "I'd appreciate having a word with you when you have a moment."

Parker studied Theo for a moment, then nodded. "I have an appointment in a few minutes, but I can see you in half an hour."

"Thanks, Captain." When he reached the doorway, Theo turned to Kit. "Keep in touch, bro."

"Ditto," Kit said.

When they were alone in the room, Parker said, "I'm going to release Ms. Merriweather into your custody. Until we get to the bottom of this, I'm going to give her some protection."

"You think she's still in danger?" Kit asked.

"I think there's a hell of a lot we don't know yet. Those thugs are hired help, and whoever is behind this may think Ms. Merriweather knows more than she does. They may send more after her. I'll assign a surveillance team twenty-four seven. But it may not be enough."

The fact that Parker was only giving voice to Kit's own thoughts wasn't very comforting. "I'll take care of her. What about Roman?"

Parker's eyebrows shot up. "I think I've extended all the courtesy to you that I'm going to, Mr. Angelis. I'm not commenting to you on an ongoing investigation. And your brother Theo isn't going to get much out of me, either." With a nod, Parker walked out into the squad room.

Kit turned to enter the interrogation room. Two strides took him to the table where Drew was still seated. He pulled her into his arms.

"What do we do now?" she asked.

"I'm taking you home."

21

As KIT PARKED in front of his aunt Cass's house and helped her out, the knots in Drew's stomach tightened. He'd said he was taking her *home*. It had only been a day, not even twenty-four hours since he'd first brought her here on that motorcycle. But every thing looked so different this time.

First of all, there was the fog. It had rolled in suddenly the way fog did in San Francisco, and now it was so thick that she could barely make out the porch steps until they reached them. The tower was completely invisible, so this time the house didn't remind her of a princess's castle.

As Kit placed a hand on her back and guided her across the width of the porch, she realized that the biggest difference this time was that she felt as if she *were* coming home.

But it wasn't her home, she reminded herself. Now that the excitement had died down and the men who'd been chasing her were behind bars, she and Kit would have to talk about what had happened between them. Ever since they'd left the police station, the cautious side of her nature had been reasserting itself.

She'd insisted that they stop at St. Jude's so that Kit

could check on Roman. Not merely because she knew that Kit would feel better once he had, but also because she was a coward.

While Kit had been talking to Mario Oliver, she'd almost convinced herself that she and Kit should slow things down a bit. Almost. That would be the smartest choice they could make at this point. Right?

Kit opened the front door, then took her hand to draw her over the threshold. Once they were both inside and the door was closed again, he raised her hand to his lips. "You're worried about something, and now that we're home, you're going to tell me what."

Home. There was that word again. "I'm worried about Roman," she said. It wasn't a total lie. She *was* worried about him. Kit had told her that the surgery had gone well, and the doctors were very positive about Roman's prognosis. But he was still sedated and unable to talk about what had happened.

"I couldn't help but feel sorry for Mr. Oliver. His two daughters are missing, and the press has latched on to the idea that Roman is guilty of kidnapping and extortion."

"He'll protect Roman. And Theo is working on the case. He's very good at what he does."

That didn't surprise her. The Angelis brothers all seemed to be very good at what they did.

The corners of Kit's mouth lifted. "With Mario's help, Theo will stonewall the police as long as he can, and he knows that Nik and I are working on it."

"Oh, there you are." Cass Angelis appeared at the head of the stairs and hurried toward them. She wore an apron and was wiping her hands on a towel. "You're a bit earlier than I expected, but everything's ready, I think." When she reached them, she took Drew's hands in hers. "You must feel relieved that the danger for you is over, my dear."

"How did you know?" Drew studied the older woman. The warmth in Cass's eyes somehow helped to ease the knot of nerves in her stomach.

Cass smiled at her. "I sometimes get a sense of things. Don't worry. The problems bothering you now will fade as soon as you make the choice the Fates are offering you."

The moment that Cass released her and turned to Kit, Drew felt an odd sense of loss.

"I hope you don't mind, but I went into your apartment and popped something in the oven for you. It's on warm, so you can eat it when you get to it." Then she beamed a smile at both of them. "I won't keep you. I know you have a lot to talk about." She wrapped each of them in a hug before she turned and hurried down the long corridor toward her apartment at the back of the house.

A lot to talk about. Cass's words echoed in Drew's mind and the knot in her stomach tightened again as she climbed the stairs. The walk down the hall to Kit's door seemed much longer than it had the last time he'd brought her here. Things had been simpler then. She hadn't known who she was and the only two problems facing her had been finding out her identity and deciding how she was going to handle the overwhelming attraction she felt for Kit. Now everything was so complicated. Her feelings for him had gone from incredible attraction to being in love with him.

There was a part of her that wanted to tell him that— probably the gun-shooting, motorcycle-riding part. However, the cautious and practical part of her felt obligated to be fair, to offer Kit a chance to slow things down, to step back a bit. To run away?

The tension inside of her increased as she stepped into Kit's apartment. Then her eyes widened in surprise. Candles flickered on the bookshelves and on the coffee table. Harp music flowed out of the sound system. "What…"

Kit smiled at her. "Aunt Cass has a romantic heart."

"Well…she's… I…" Because she found it hard to think when Kit was looking at her in that way, she glanced away and forced herself to walk toward the windows. The fog was so thick that it seemed like a solid mass pressing against the window pane. What was she going to tell him?

She was slipping away from him. Kit knew it in the same way he had "sensed" Drew's visit to his office the night before. That had been less than twenty-four hours ago.

Amazing. He'd known her less than a day, and he *knew* that she was the woman for him, the woman he was fated for. He just had to persuade her to be as sure of that as he was.

Pushing down fear, he closed the door behind him and waited. It wasn't what he wanted to do. He wanted more than anything to go to her and to take her in his arms. But his experience as a fisherman and as a private investigator had taught him that patience nearly always paid off.

Finally, she turned to him. Her hands were clasped tightly in front of her. "The music is lovely."

"The harpist is Greek, and she's a favorite of Aunt Cass's. We all grew up listening to her music."

Drew nodded and twisted her fingers. "That's not what I want to talk about."

Kit waited.

"I want to thank you for saving my life."

Anger flared in Kit, but he shoved it down. Every time he thought of her standing there, holding the gun… He shoved that image away, too. "It could just as easily have gone the other way. Given the chance, you would have shot that bastard and saved *my* life. So let's agree that it was a mutual saving." Unable to prevent himself, he took a step forward. "Drew—"

"No—" she held up a hand "—let me have my say. Things happen to people when they're involved in the kind of stressful situations that we've been involved in."

And those things are going to keep on happening. Kit bit his tongue to keep from saying the words aloud. "Good things happened."

"Yes. But you don't know anything about me." She held her hand up again. "We're so different. My life has been so easy compared to yours. You've had to work all your life."

When she paused, Kit said, "I know a lot about you."

"What? That I'm a sex…bunny? I didn't have any idea that I was like that."

His eyebrows shot up. "A sex bunny?"

She waved a hand. "I want to make love to you every time I see you. I want to make love to you right now."

"I'd be happy to oblige you."

She took a step toward him, then whirled and began to pace. "It's not enough. I'm mean, it's great, the sex is fabulous, but…"

"I know what you mean."

She ran a hand through her hair and continued to pace. "You should know that I was a very spoiled, privileged child. My parents gave me everything—well, everything they wanted me to have. The best schools, the best clothes. They expected me to go into the family business, and I didn't."

"I know the feeling."

She looked at him. "Maybe you do. When I went into fashion design in college, they were disappointed. But when I graduated, they offered me the money to start my own store."

"You didn't take it."

She shook her head. "I knew that they were doing it to humor me. My father would have thought of it as an investment for the future. They were sure I would fail, and then they would caringly and gently push me into the family business where they could continue to direct my life."

"So you moved to the other side of the continent to make it on your own."

"Yes. I was afraid that I *would* fail and that I would let them find a place for me in the family business and take care of me for the rest of my life. So I ran away. That's where we're different. I'm a coward and you're not."

"A coward?" It took all of his control, but Kit managed to stay where he was and keep his voice steady. "It wasn't a coward who moved out here to San Francisco. It wasn't a coward who shot that thug at St. Peter's. And tell me that you wouldn't have put a bullet in that other bastard a few hours ago if you could have gotten a clear shot."

"I never stood up to the Dragon Lady."

"I think you would have."

"Really?"

"Would you have let her fire you?"

Drew thought for a moment, then slowly shook her head. "No. I would have quit first." Her chin lifted. "And I would have taken all my designs with me."

"See?" Kit smiled. "You're not a coward." He'd taken a step toward her when his cell phone rang. "Yes?"

Drew studied him as he listened intently to whoever was calling. Her plan was to tell him that they should back off from one another, slow things down a bit. Wasn't that the act of a coward?

He was so many things that she wasn't. And it didn't just have to do with their backgrounds. She was cautious, he was impulsive. She was serious. He could be outrageously funny. She operated best with a plan. He talked about plans but preferred to improvise. They shouldn't fit.

Yet somehow they did. They fit perfectly. She thought of Cass's words—"The problems facing you will fade away as soon as you make the choice that the Fates are offering you."

The Fates were offering her Kit. Could it be that simple? That right?

Kit frowned as he pocketed his cell phone.

"Trouble?" Drew asked.

"Yes. I had this feeling all day long that there was this other shoe about to drop. That was Theo. He met with Parker and found out that the police lab has identified both Roman's and Sadie Oliver's fingerprints on the ransom notes."

She moved to him then. "They'll arrest Roman, won't they?"

"Yes." He ran a hand through his hair. "It doesn't make sense. Roman's not a stupid man. If he sent those notes, he wouldn't have left fingerprints on them."

"Someone is trying to frame him."

Anger and frustration moved through him. "And they're doing a hell of a good job."

"You'll figure it out," Drew said. "You'll work with your brothers and figure it all out."

Stung by her use of the word *you'll,* Kit stared at her.

Fear joined the other emotions coursing through him, and he felt his earlier resolve melting away. To hell with giving her time. To hell with being patient. He grabbed her by the arms. "*We'll* figure it out. You're part of the team now."

When she started to speak, he gave her a little shake. "I know what you're going to say. You're going to tell me that we should be practical and cautious and slow things down. That maybe we should back away from one another and get a little perspective. And I thought I could go along with that. I'm a patient man. At least, I've always thought of myself that way. But I can't wait." He gave her another shake. "I love you."

He kissed her then, hard. It took only a moment for her to soften, and he immediately gentled the kiss. He shoved down the urge to pull her to the floor and show her what he was feeling and what he really needed. When he finally drew away, they were both trembling, and Kit took a careful step back. "I love making love with you. But I want more from you than that. I want everything."

With a sigh, he pulled her close again and rested his forehead on the top of her head. "And I'm sorry. We can take it slow if that's what—"

"No." The sound was muffled but distinct enough to have him pulling back once more.

"Drew—"

She pressed her fingers against his lips. "Don't I deserve the right to tell you what I want?"

His eyes narrowed as he studied her face. "What?"

"You were right about what I was planning on telling you. I thought I had to be fair and give you a choice. But I don't want to be fair. Your aunt Cass is right. Whatever has happened this weekend, perhaps because of it, the

Fates have offered me a choice. And I'm going to make it. I don't care whether it's fair to you or not. I love you. I want you. Therefore, I choose you."

Unable to speak, Kit did a much better thing. He kissed her again. When he dew back this time, he lifted her high and swung her around. "Excellent choice."

They were both laughing when he set her back on her feet, pulled the scarf loose from her waist and dropped it to the floor. "It's only fair to tell you that the back of my neck is tingling." He reached behind her to pull down the zipper of her sundress. "So I have a good idea of where this is going to lead. Want to know?"

"I'm not a psychic, but I have a good idea, too." She struggled with the snap on his jeans as her dress pooled at her feet. She met his eyes then. "I'm not Greek, either. Is that going to be a problem for your family?"

Kit seemed to consider it for a moment. Then he flashed the dimples. "Everyone is entitled to one flaw. We'll work on it. It'll take time, though. A lot of time."

They were both laughing as they rid themselves of the rest of their clothes and sank to the floor.

In her tower room, Cass smiled as she stared into her crystals. Harp music filled the air, mingling with the scent of burning laurel leaves. Kit and Drew had made their choices and accepted their fate. But there were many dangers that still lay ahead for Nik and Theo. The colored mists in the faceted stones swirled and then cleared. Oh, yes, Cass thought. There would be the choice of love for them, too—if they had the courage to make it.

* * * * *

*For a sneak peek at Nik's story—THE COP—
just turn the page.*

1

J. C. RILEY WASN'T SURE how much longer she could stay hidden in the depths of the priest's cupboard. Patience was not her strong suit. Even as a child, she'd hated to wait for anything. Had enough time passed for that awful man with the snake eyes to go away? He'd shot Father Mike and then turned his gun on her.

Just thinking about it made her stomach growl. She was absolutely starving. She always got ravenously hungry whenever she was scared or nervous. She'd made the 9-1-1 call eons ago. Shouldn't the police have arrived by now?

She thought she'd heard a siren, but that had been a while ago. And it could have been wishful thinking. She wasn't even sure how long she'd been hiding. She'd tried to say a rosary—something she hadn't done in years. How long had that taken? Five minutes? Ten? She needed to check on Father Mike and find out how badly he was hurt. The only reason she hadn't was that she couldn't do him much good if the snake-eyed man with the gun was still out there.

It was too dark to check her watch. If she could just hear something… Whatever Father Mike's vestments were made of, they certainly blocked out sound. The police could be here right now, and she wouldn't know it.

What she did know was that her fear of the snake-eyed man was gradually being replaced by her fear of being confined in a small space. And Father Mike's cupboard gave new meaning to the word *confined*. She felt as if she were buried in vestments. The incense lingering on them had grown cloying. Keep calm, she told herself. But she could feel her heart beating faster and faster.

As the urge to bolt began to grow, J.C. forced herself to imagine Snake Eyes looking at her—searching the rectory, then returning to the sacristy. At any moment he could fling open the cupboard and start plowing through the garments.

She was a sitting duck. Well, there was no sense in making it easy for him.

Slowly she burrowed her way toward the front of the cupboard, holding her breath each time one vestment rubbed against another. When she reached the door, she discovered that in her rush to hide herself, she hadn't closed it completely. Pressing her face to the narrow opening, she peered through it and fear bubbled through again.

A man stood over the body of the dead man. He had his back to her, but she knew he wasn't Snake Eyes. This man was taller, broader. Snake Eyes' hair had been slicked back close to his head because of the ski mask. This man's hair was dark, curly and unruly. But she could sense just as much danger emanating from him as she had from Snake Eyes.

He was wearing a tank top that fit snugly over bronze-colored skin. As he began to move slowly around the dead man, she caught her first glimpse of his face and, for a moment she stared, fascinated. He reminded her of the Greek gods that she'd read about in books. One in particular, she thought as she searched for the name. Adonis? Except that Adonis hadn't been a god—just the human lover of two very powerful goddesses, Persephone and Aphrodite, who fought over him constantly. She was never quite sure why the story fascinated her so—it was definitely a male fantasy. Personally, she'd yet to meet a man worth fighting someone over.

J.C. gave herself a mental shake. This man might not be Snake Eyes, but he might very well be the man who'd fired those other shots she'd heard. As she continued to study him, she decided he wasn't as pretty as Adonis had been—in the pictures, anyway. This man was more... rugged-looking. His nose was quite straight. Taking in the sharp slash of cheekbone and the strong line of his jaw, she thought of a warrior—the kind of man who would lead armies into war—and win. That didn't at all explain why she had the oddest urge to touch his face—to feel the planes and angles of those bones beneath her hands.

What was up with that? she thought with a frown. Warriors had never been her type.

But then, when it came to men, she really hadn't had much experience determining her type. The kind of men her dad and step-mom wanted her to date might as well be clones of each other, successful young professional males with the right kind of family backgrounds. She found them almost as boring as the temperamental prima donnas she'd met when she'd trained at the American Culinary Institute.

The man in front of her had circled the body so that he was standing with his back to her again, and she caught herself noticing the way his threadbare jeans molded his butt. Good Lord, she wanted to touch that, too.

Had Aphrodite and Persephone felt this almost overwhelming urge to get their hands on Adonis the first time they'd seen him?

Whoa! J.C. reined in her thoughts again. A vivid imagination had always plagued her as a child, but she'd never reacted in quite this physical a way to a man before. Just looking at Mr. Adonis made her palms itch.

For the first time, she noticed the gun and her throat went dry. It was tucked into the waistband of his jeans—right above his exceptional-looking…

Stop it, she scolded herself. This man could be working with Snake Eyes. She could very well be looking at a killer. A ruthless, cold-blooded killer.

In that very instant, he whirled on her and she found herself looking down the barrel of a very big gun.

"Open the door slowly and keep your hands where I can see them. Don't make me shoot you."

"Who in the hell are you?" Nik Angelis asked as a tiny redhead stepped out of the cupboard.

"Who are you?" she countered.

"I'm a cop, so I get to ask the questions." She didn't look like she'd played a part of the carnage in the church, but his thumbs had begun to prick the moment he'd stepped into the sacristy. That always told him that something was about to go down. But it didn't sit well with him that it had taken him so long to sense her presence in that cupboard.

"Who are you?" he asked again.

"I'm the caterer for the wedding. Now it's your turn."

Nik narrowed his eyes. For a little bit of a thing she had guts. Under other circumstances, he might have enjoyed it, but the church was getting crowded. The EMTs were dealing with Father Mike and Roman Oliver. He'd arranged for both of them to be transported to the new St. Jude's Trauma Center and he'd sent the first crime-scene team to the choir loft because he'd wanted a few minutes alone with the body in the sacristy. He'd called his captain, and D. C. Parker would want a full report as soon as he disentangled himself from some big charity ball he was attending.

"What's your name?" Nik asked.

"You know, you don't look like a cop. Those clothes are a bit casual even for a dress-down Friday. Do policemen even have casual-dress days?" She lowered one of her hands and held it out to him, palm up. "Show me some ID."

For such a small package, she certainly had a big mouth. Nike swept his gaze over her. She couldn't be more than five foot two, but her stance and the way she was looking at him radiated enough attitude for a woman twice her size. She had her hair twisted up on her head, but a few red curls had escaped. Her ruffled white shirt was tucked into black pants that showcased surprisingly long legs. His gaze lingered on them for a moment before he shifted his attention back to her face. That was when he noticed her eyes. They were green and direct and, for a moment, he saw nothing else.

"Well? You do carry ID, don't you?"

Annoyance and something else moved through Nik, as he forced himself to blink and break eye contact. Then he gave her his cop smile, the one his partner Dinah said looked like a sneer. "Dream on, sweetheart. Let me make this as clear as possible. I not only ask the questions, I give the orders. Turn around, put your hands flat against the door of the cupboard and spread your legs."

There was a beat before she did what he asked, and he couldn't prevent the ripple of admiration that moved through him. He'd always been a bit of a sucker for a woman with guts. He was halfway through patting her down when he realized that he'd made a huge mistake. He was actually enjoying the feel of those tight little muscles, soft curves and slim bones beneath his palms. Dammit, he was a professional. This crime scene needed his full attention.

The moment he straightened, she whirled to face him. In that moment when their bodies brushed against each other, a ripple of heat ran through him. What in the hell—

He took a quick step back, but he could tell by the way her green eyes darkened that she'd felt it, too.

"Who the hell are you?" he asked.

She lifted her chin. "I told you. I'm the caterer."

"Detective Angelis?"

Nike recognized the voice of the young officer he'd left with Father Mike, but he kept his gaze on the redhead. "Now you know *my* name. What's yours?"

"I'm J. C. Riley. I made the 9-1-1 call, and I want—"

Nik held up a hand to cut her off. "What is it, officer?"

"Sir, they're about to take the priest away."

Nik tucked his gun into the waistband of his jeans, then grasped the little redhead around the waist, lifted her and plunked her on the counter. "Stay put, pipsqueak. I'll take care of you later."

* * * * *

THE ROYAL HOUSE OF NIROLI
Always passionate, always proud.

The richest royal family in the world—united by blood and passion, torn apart by deceit and desire.

Nestled in the azure blue of the Mediterranean Sea, the majestic island of Niroli has prospered for centuries. The Fierezza men have worn the crown with passion and pride since ancient times. But now, as the king's health declines and his two sons have been tragically killed, the crown is in jeopardy.

The clock is ticking—a new heir must be found before the king is forced to abdicate. By royal decree the internationally scattered members of the Fierezza family are summoned to claim their destiny. But any person who takes the throne must do so according to The Rules of the Royal House of Niroli. Soon secrets and rivalries emerge as the descendents of this ancient royal line vie for position and power. Only a true Fierezza can become ruler—a person dedicated to their country, their people…and their eternal love!

Each month starting in July 2007,
Harlequin Presents is delighted to bring you
an exciting installment from
THE ROYAL HOUSE OF NIROLI,
in which you can follow the epic search
for the true Nirolian king.
Eight heirs, eight romances, eight fantastic stories!

Here's your chance to enjoy a sneak preview of the first book delivered to you by royal decree….

FIVE minutes later she was standing immobile in front of the study's window, her original purpose of coming in forgotten, as she stared in shocked horror at the envelope she was holding. Waves of heat followed by icy chill surged through her body. She could hardly see the address now through her blurred vision, but the crest on its left-hand front corner stood out, its *royal* crest, followed by the address: *HRH Prince Marco of Niroli….*

She didn't hear Marco's key in the apartment door, she didn't even hear him calling out her name. Her shock was so great that nothing could penetrate it. It encased her in a kind of bubble, which only concentrated the torment of what she was suffering and branded it on her brain so that it could never be forgotten. It was only finally pierced by the sudden opening of the study door as Marco walked in.

"Welcome home, *Your Highness.* I suppose I ought to curtsy." She waited, praying that he would laugh and tell her that she had got it all wrong, that the envelope she was holding, addressing him as Prince Marco of Niroli, was some silly mistake. But like a tiny candle flame shivering vulnerably in the dark, her hope trembled fearfully. And then the look in Marco's eyes extinguished it as cruelly as a hand placed callously over a dying person's face to stem their last breath.

"Give that to me," he demanded, taking the envelope from her.

"It's too late, Marco," Emily told him brokenly. "I know the truth now…" She dug her teeth in her lower lip to try to force back her own pain.

"You had no right to go through my desk," Marco shot back at her furiously, full of loathing at being caught off guard and forced into a position in which he was in the wrong, making him determined to find something he could accuse Emily of. "I trusted you…."

Emily could hardly believe what she was hearing. "No, you didn't trust me, Marco, and you didn't trust me because you knew that I couldn't trust you. And you knew that because you're a liar, and liars don't trust people because they know that they themselves cannot be trusted." She not only felt sick, she also felt as though she could hardly breathe. "You are Prince Marco of Niroli… How could you not tell me who you are and still live with me as intimately as we have lived together?" she demanded brokenly.

"Stop being so ridiculously dramatic," Marco demanded fiercely. "You are making too much of the situation."

"*Too much?*" Emily almost screamed the words at him. "When were you going to tell me, Marco? Perhaps you just planned to walk away without telling me anything? After all, what do my feelings matter to you?"

"Of course they matter." Marco stopped her sharply. "And it was in part to protect them, and you, that I decided not to inform you when my grandfather first announced that he intended to step down from the throne and hand it on to me."

"To protect me?" Emily nearly choked on her fury. "Hand on the throne? No wonder you told me when you first took me to bed that all you wanted was sex. You *knew* that was the only kind of relationship there could ever be between us! You *knew* that one day you would be Niroli's king. No doubt you are expected to marry a princess. Is she picked out for you already, your *royal* bride?"

* * * * *

Look for THE FUTURE KING'S PREGNANT
MISTRESS
by Penny Jordan in July 2007,
from Harlequin Presents,
available wherever books are sold.

nocturne™

**DON'T MISS THE RIVETING CONCLUSION
TO THE RAINTREE TRILOGY**

RAINTREE: SANCTUARY

by *New York Times* bestselling author

BEVERLY BARTON

Mercy, guardian of the Raintree
homeplace, takes a stand against
the Ansara wizards to battle for
the Clan's future.

*On sale July,
wherever books are sold.*

SNRT2

Silhouette®

Romantic
SUSPENSE

**Sparked by Danger,
Fueled by Passion.**

Mission: Impassioned

A brand-new miniseries begins with

My Spy

By *USA TODAY* bestselling author

Marie Ferrarella

She had to trust him with her life....
It was the most daring mission of Joshua Lazlo's
career: rescuing the prime minister of England's
daughter from a gang of cold-blooded kidnappers.
But nothing prepared the shadowy secret agent
for a fiery woman whose touch ignited something
far more dangerous.

My Spy

#1472

Available July 2007 wherever you buy books!

Visit Silhouette Books at www.eHarlequin.com   SRS27542

Do you know
a real-life heroine?

Nominate her for the Harlequin
More Than Words award.

Each year Harlequin Enterprises honors five
ordinary women for their extraordinary
commitment to their community.

Each recipient of the Harlequin More Than Words
award receives a $10,000 donation from Harlequin
to advance the work of her chosen charity. And five
of Harlequin's most acclaimed authors donate their
time and creative talents to writing a novella inspired
by the award recipients. The More Than Words
anthology is published annually in October and all
proceeds benefit causes of concern to women.

HARLEQUIN

More Than Words™

**For more details or to nominate
a woman you know please visit**

www.HarlequinMoreThanWords.com

HARLEQUIN®

Mediterranean NIGHTS™

Experience the glamour and elegance of cruising the high seas with a new 12-book series....

MEDITERRANEAN NIGHTS

Coming in July 2007...

SCENT OF A WOMAN

by

Joanne Rock

When Danielle Chevalier is invited to an exclusive conference aboard *Alexandra's Dream,* she knows it will mean good things for her struggling fragrance company. But her dreams get a setback when she meets Adam Burns, a representative from a large American conglomerate.

Danielle is charmed by the brusque American— until she finds out he means to compete with her bid for the opportunity that will save her family business!

www.eHarlequin.com

HM38961

REQUEST YOUR FREE BOOKS!

2 FREE NOVELS PLUS 2 FREE GIFTS!

HARLEQUIN®

Blaze®

Red-hot reads!

YES! Please send me 2 FREE Harlequin® Blaze® novels and my 2 FREE gifts. After receiving them, if I don't wish to receive any more books, I can return the shipping statement marked "cancel." If I don't cancel, I will receive 6 brand-new novels every month and be billed just $3.99 per book in the U.S., or $4.47 per book in Canada, plus 25¢ shipping and handling per book and applicable taxes, if any*. That's a savings of at least 15% off the cover price! I understand that accepting the 2 free books and gifts places me under no obligation to buy anything. I can always return a shipment and cancel at any time. Even if I never buy another book from Harlequin, the two free books and gifts are mine to keep forever.

151 HDN EF3W   351 HDN EF3X

Name	(PLEASE PRINT)	
Address		Apt.
City	State/Prov.	Zip/Postal Code

Signature (if under 18, a parent or guardian must sign)

Mail to the **Harlequin Reader Service**®:
IN U.S.A.: P.O. Box 1867, Buffalo, NY 14240-1867
IN CANADA: P.O. Box 609, Fort Erie, Ontario. L2A 5X3

Not valid to current Harlequin Blaze subscribers.

**Want to try two free books from another line?
Call 1-800-873-8635 or visit www.morefreebooks.com.**

* Terms and prices subject to change without notice. NY residents add applicable sales tax. Canadian residents will be charged applicable provincial taxes and GST. This offer is limited to one order per household. All orders subject to approval. Credit or debit balances in a customer's account(s) may be offset by any other outstanding balance owed by or to the customer. Please allow 4 to 6 weeks for delivery.

Your Privacy: Harlequin is committed to protecting your privacy. Our Privacy Policy is available online at www.eHarlequin.com or upon request from the Reader Service. From time to time we make our lists of customers available to reputable firms who may have a product or service of interest to you. If you would prefer we not share your name and address, please check here. ☐

HB07

THE GARRISONS
A brand-new family saga begins with

THE CEO'S SCANDALOUS AFFAIR
BY ROXANNE ST. CLAIRE

Eldest son Parker Garrison is preoccupied running his Miami hotel empire and dealing with his recently deceased father's secret second family. Since he has little time to date, taking his superefficient assistant to a charity event should have been a simple plan. Until passion takes them beyond business.

Don't miss any of the six exciting titles in THE GARRISONS continuity, beginning in July. Only from Silhouette Desire.

THE CEO'S SCANDALOUS AFFAIR
#1807

Available July 2007.

Visit Silhouette Books at www.eHarlequin.com   SD76807

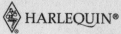 **HARLEQUIN®**

COMING NEXT MONTH

#333 MEN AT WORK Karen Kendall/Cindi Myers/Colleen Collins
Hot Summer Anthology
When these construction hotties pose for a charity calendar, more than a few pulses go through the roof! Add in Miami's steamy temperatures that beg a man to peel off his shirt and the result? Three sexy stories in one *very* hot collection. Don't miss it!

#334 THE ULTIMATE BITE Crystal Green
Extreme
A year ago he came to her—a vampire in need, seducing her with an incredible bite, an intimate bite…a forgettable bite? Haunted by the sensuality of that night, Kim's been searching for Stephen ever since. Imagine her surprise when she realizes he doesn't even remember her. And his surprise…when he discovers that Kim will do anything to become his Ultimate Bite…

#335 TAKEN Tori Carrington
The Bad Girls Club, Bk. 1
Seline Sanborn is a con artist. And power broker Ryder Blackwell is her handsome mark. An incredible one-night stand has Ryder falling, *hard*. But what will he do when he wakes up to find the angel in his bed gone…along with a chunk of his company's funds?

#336 THE COP Cara Summers
Tall, Dark…and Dangerously Hot! Bk. 2
Off-duty detective Nik Angelis is the first responder at a wedding-turned-murder-scene. The only witness is a fiery redhead who needs his protection—but *wants* his rock-hard body. Nik aims to be professional, but a man can take only so much….

#337 GHOSTS AND ROSES Kelley St. John
The Sexth Sense, Bk. 2
Gage Vicknair has been dreaming—incredible erotic visions—about a mysterious brown-eyed beauty. He's desperate to meet her and turn those dreams into reality. Only, he doesn't expect a ghost, a woman who was murdered, to be able to help him find her. Or that he's going to have to save the woman of his dreams from a similar fate….

#338 SHE DID A BAD, BAD THING Stephanie Bond
Million Dollar Secrets, Bk. 1
Mild-mannered makeup artist Jane Kurtz has always wished she had the nerve to go for things she wants. Like her neighbor Perry Brewer. So when she wins the lottery, she sees her chance—she's going to Vegas for the ultimate bad-girl makeover. Perry won't know what hit him. But he'll know soon. Because Perry's in Vegas, too….

www.eHarlequin.com

HBCNM0607